THE UNEXPECTED
HEIRESS

By the Author

Writ of Love

The Unexpected Heiress

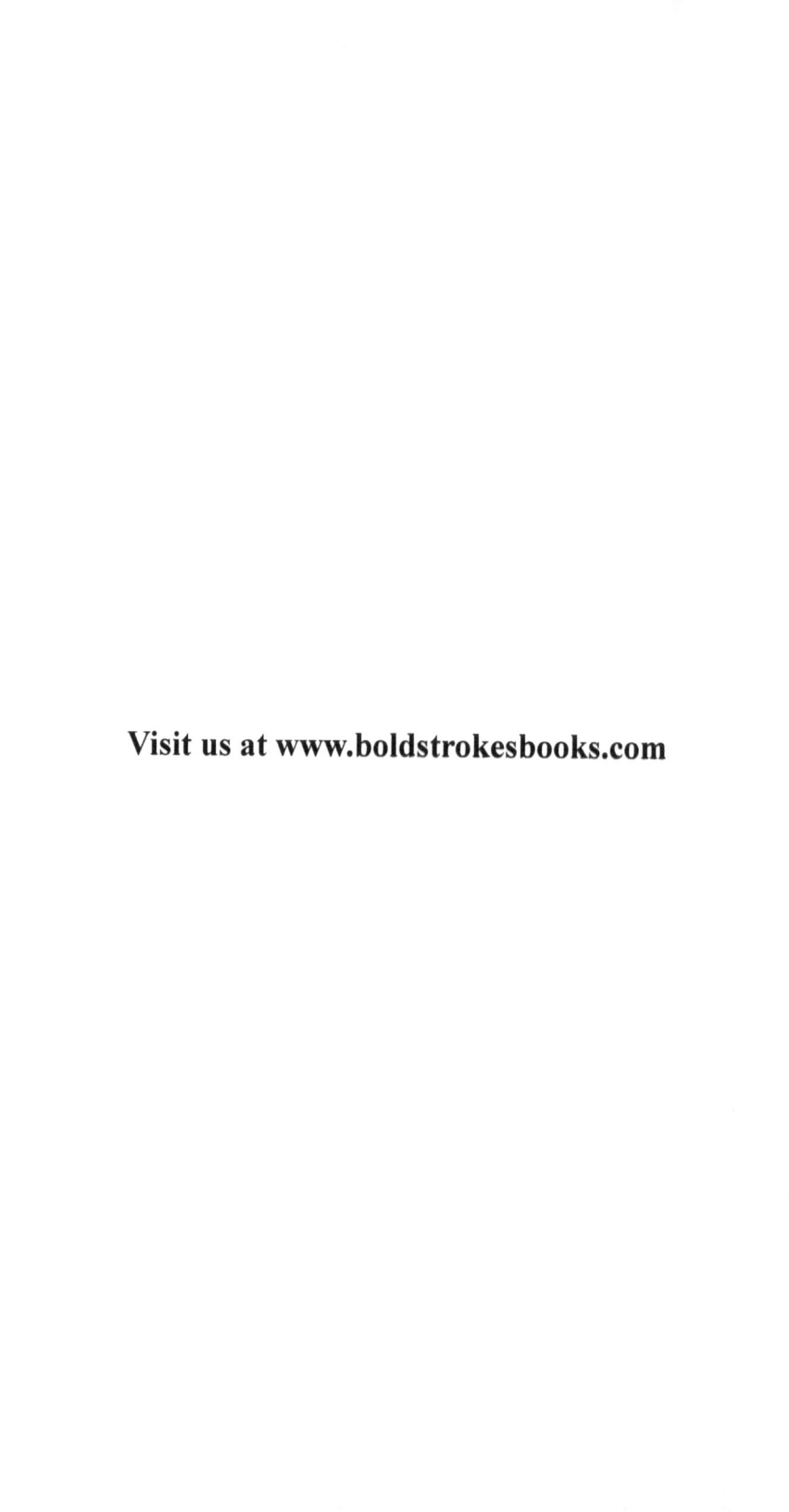

Visit us at www.boldstrokesbooks.com

THE UNEXPECTED HEIRESS

by

Cassidy Crane

2025

ISBN 13: 978-1-63679-833-2

This Trade Paperback Original Is Published By
Bold Strokes Books, Inc.
P.O. Box 249
Valley Falls, NY 12185

First Edition: August 2025

Credits

Editor: Barbara Ann Wright
Production Design: Stacia Seaman
Cover Design by Inkspiral Design

Acknowledgments

Thank you to everyone at Bold Strokes Books, especially my editor, Barbara Ann Wright.

Thank you to my friends and family for their love and support.

Thank you to my cats for the avant-garde editorial suggestions they made by walking across my keyboard. I didn't use any of them this time, but maybe they'll make the next book.

Most of all, thank you to my wife. You're simply the best.

For my wife.

CHAPTER ONE

Geneva, Switzerland, July 1929

Clara Cooper wondered what the penalty for murder was in Switzerland. Even if it was death, it might have been worth it. She had borne Aunt Matilda's complaints for three weeks already, and there were still another three weeks of the trip to go. Perhaps her aunt could meet with a tragic accident, like falling down the stairs or drowning in the river.

"Clara, dear, do stop scowling like that. You'll get wrinkles, and you're having a hard enough time finding a husband as it is. Back in my day, you'd be considered an old maid by now."

The background noise of the hotel restaurant rose to a din as Clara wrung her handkerchief in lieu of her aunt's neck. Could a teacup full of cyanide pass for an accident? The thought gave her a modicum of comfort as she hiked an insincere smile onto her face. "Things are different now, Aunt Matilda. There are respectable careers for women. We can even vote." She couldn't risk pushing back too much, but she'd had more of her aunt's nagging than she could bear. She scanned the room to see if there was anything worth drawing here, but the hotel was rather drab, and nothing was particularly inspiring.

"And why any woman would care about that, I can't imagine," Aunt Matilda said scornfully, picking up her soup spoon. "*Tuh.* You ought to be thinking about marriage and children, not working and certainly not *voting*. Your parents have been far too soft on you. Why, by the time I was your age, your cousin Harry was already in kindergarten, and I don't think I even knew who the president was."

By the skin of her teeth, Clara managed to keep her eyeroll to herself. She hadn't been able to vote in the 1924 election, not being twenty-one yet at the time, but she had eagerly accompanied her mother to the polls this past November.

It was all well and good for Aunt Matilda to scoff at the idea of a woman having a career, but Clara didn't have the luxury of inherited wealth. Realistically, marriage was her best option if she didn't want to resort to being a housemaid or factory worker. She had no real skills to speak of that would be useful in a professional setting, nor did she have any desire to rely on handouts from snobby relatives like Aunt Matilda. Those always came with strings attached, hence her having to endure Aunt Matilda's barbs for this entire journey.

Try as she might, Clara couldn't bring herself to strive for the life the Aunt Matildas of the world believed she should have had. The thought of settling down with one of the young men her family had paraded her in front of with increasing desperation filled her with dread. None of them had particularly interested her, and she was under no delusions about her appeal to them, either. She had sprouted up in grade school, and even in high school, her six-foot frame had towered over many of the boys in her class. Her shoulders were too broad, her hair a mousy brown, and her face could charitably be described as plain. Aunt Matilda, notably lacking in charity, had been overheard referring to her niece as *a most unfortunate-looking girl* on more than one occasion. Combined with her family's lack of money, it was little wonder that she was still unmarried at twenty-five.

She spooned soup into her mouth as she glumly pondered the fact that this trip was almost certainly the most exciting thing that would ever happen to her. Her father's job teaching art at a private boys' school kept a roof over their heads, but his estrangement from her wealthy grandfather before her birth had taken a toll on the family finances. Her parents could never have afforded to send her on this journey, and when they died, there would be no legacy large enough to allow her to live independently.

She felt a twinge of unease when she thought about the future and her utter lack of prospects, but that was a problem to be dealt with when she got home. For now, she was going to wring every moment of enjoyment she possibly could out of this opportunity.

She wanted to travel, to draw and paint, to control her own life.

She had seen so little of the world; outside of occasional day trips into Boston, she had barely left Willoughby, her sleepy Massachusetts hometown. Accompanying Aunt Matilda on this voyage had been the opportunity of a lifetime, even though it meant putting up with her aunt's company.

Despite the wonderful experiences she'd had already, she kept hoping that something truly magical would happen on the trip. Maybe she'd meet a dashing Frenchman who would sweep her off her feet in a way the boys at home never did, or she'd stumble upon a dramatic crime like in one of Agatha Christie's novels and get to assist a famous detective. Not that she could think of a single real-life famous detective, but she lived in hope.

In only a few short hours, they would depart on a cruise down the Rhône River. It was the perfect opportunity for just such an adventure, ten days on a small ship sailing through Auvergne and Provence.

CHAPTER TWO

Adeline Barnes hurried down the starboard deck, anxious to get to the gangplank before the first guests arrived. The well-heeled passengers would look for even the most minute of errors as an excuse to complain, or even worse, not leave a tip. She scanned the passenger manifest one last time, all thirty-six names already burned into her brain.

When the passengers started arriving, she kept an eye out for the most likely prospects she had flagged from the manifest: Miss Hester Windermere, an English heiress; Mrs. Matilda Cooper, a wealthy American widow; and her niece, Miss Clara Cooper. As far as Addie could tell, Clara Cooper had no money of her own to speak of, but she might prove a valuable ally if Matilda Cooper turned out to be a viable target.

If only Eva had updated her will sooner, Addie thought uselessly for the thousandth time. Instead, here she was working as the stewardess on a tourist boat traveling up and down the Rhône, hoping against hope that she'd find her next Eva. Well, not another Eva; the pain of her death had nearly destroyed Addie, and she was never going to put herself in such a position again. Far better to find some well-to-do woman who wanted a pretty young thing by her side for a while and was willing to pay generously for the privilege. There was no need for emotion to enter the picture.

Several passengers arrived, and Addie plastered on the well-practiced smile she always used to greet them: eager to be of service but not obsequious. As a stewardess, she walked a difficult line, unique from any of the other ship's staff. She wasn't quite a servant, but neither was she the passengers' social equal.

She was there to cater to their every need, whether it was arranging a tour at the next port of call or making sure their pillows had been properly fluffed. Sometimes that included less-defined things that they didn't even know to ask for: smoothing over disputes between passengers and staff or ensuring that a shy traveler didn't spend the whole trip dining alone. She rarely ate with the passengers, but she prided herself on a particular form of "matchmaking" between acquaintances.

Two women walked gingerly up the gangplank, and Addie stepped forward to greet them.

"—simply *absurd*," the older woman was declaring loudly to the younger one. "Oh, hello."

"Welcome aboard," Addie said warmly. "I'm Miss Barnes, the stewardess. I am here to help you with anything you might need. May I have your names?"

"Cooper. Mrs. Henry Cooper and Miss Clara Cooper," the older woman stated. "You don't know how good it is to hear another American. Civilization at last. Thank heavens we've made it. These Europeans have a very peculiar idea of modern amenities, haven't they? *Tuh.* Even when we were in England, I didn't expect it to be quite so *foreign.*"

She carried on for at least five minutes in this vein as Addie tried to vary her facial expressions enough to seem like she was listening. Inwardly, she was crossing Mrs. Cooper off her list. She could barely stand a brief conversation with the woman; even if she was a millionaire, Addie didn't think she could tolerate her as a lover.

"Clara, stand up straight," Mrs. Cooper barked at her niece once she had finished her lecture on the dangers of encountering foreigners in their own countries.

Clara Cooper's cheeks reddened, and she avoided Addie's gaze as she straightened herself up to her full height, looking as if she'd like nothing more than to turn invisible. With her long frame, she towered over both her aunt and Addie. Her frumpy bun and old-fashioned dress weren't doing her any favors. Addie itched to do her hair more fashionably and show her how to apply makeup that would flatter her bone structure and show off her rich brown eyes.

Addie felt a wave of sympathy for the gawky, awkward young woman and donned her most charming smile as she said, "I'm pleased to meet you, Miss Cooper. It'll be a pleasure having you aboard."

Clara sputtered out a thank-you, meeting Addie's eyes this time and blushing still further. She turned to look at Addie as a deckhand led her and her aunt to their staterooms, smiling shyly over her shoulder.

Addie made a mental note to pay extra attention to Clara Cooper during the trip; she was clearly starved for company aside from her aunt, who had probably beaten her down. If things didn't work out with Miss Windermere, maybe Addie should turn her attention to Clara instead. A fling with Addie could be just the thing to bring Clara out of her shell and boost her confidence. She'd seen the way Clara had looked at her. It would practically be an act of charity, Addie thought as she glanced at her clipboard once again.

Miss Windermere finally arrived, her fox fur stole a pop of color atop her well-cut beige pantsuit as she marched confidently up the gangplank. Her maid and a fleet of porters scurried behind her, trying to keep up while hauling teetering stacks of suitcases and hat boxes.

Addie surreptitiously patted her hair as Miss Windermere approached, knowing she needed to put her best foot forward now. This was it, her last chance on this voyage. Otherwise, she'd have to wait a month until they picked up new passengers in Marseille and hope for the best. She had primped in front of the mirror for an hour before the passengers began arriving, getting her makeup just right, carefully fastening the lapis lazuli earrings Eva had given her that brought out the vibrant blue of her eyes.

Her efforts had evidently paid off; once Miss Windermere's eyes landed on her, a pleased smirk took over her face, and she halted her brisk movements. "Why, hello there. Hester Windermere," she purred, offering a well-manicured hand for Addie to shake. She caressed the back of Addie's hand ever so lightly before letting go. Her dark hair was styled in a chic bob, her rich brown eyes bright with interest.

Jackpot. Miss Windermere struck her as the bold type who preferred to be the pursuer, so she batted her eyelashes and smiled coyly as she introduced herself. "Please allow me to show you to your cabin," Addie said, waving off the deckhand who was waiting for that purpose.

"Am I the last to arrive?" Miss Windermere asked.

"Yes, you are," Addie said.

"Jolly good," Miss Windermere said. "I can't abide waiting around for the slowcoaches to show up."

The listed departure time was half an hour ago, but Addie refrained from commenting that, from a certain perspective, Miss Windermere herself was the slowcoach. Instead, she pointed out the various features and amenities of the riverboat as they made their way to the luxury suite Miss Windermere had booked.

Addie herself had given it a once-over before the passengers arrived, making sure everything was made up perfectly and adding a vase of fresh flowers to the dresser. Miss Windermere examined the stateroom, nodding approvingly as the finger she ran along the top of the door frame came away clean of dust.

"It's a bit cramped, but it'll do for a short while," Miss Windermere said. Addie wondered how many times her own crew cabin, shared with several other girls, would fit in here. At least four times.

"I'm very glad to hear it," Addie said. "Do let me know if there's anything I can do for you to make your voyage more pleasurable. Anything at all."

She could feel Miss Windermere's eyes on her like a hawk watching a rabbit. Most of her previous lovers had preferred the shy, ingenue type, and she slipped back into the role almost effortlessly. She waited a beat before meeting her gaze, almost immediately looking away again.

"What a charming girl you are. I intend to take you up on that," Miss Windermere said with a grin. "For now, leave me alone to settle in. I'll see you later tonight."

Addie nodded and briskly left the room. That had gone well. Miss Windermere was clearly interested. As long as Addie didn't get impatient and push too hard, she might well be able to parlay it into money, gifts, or maybe even a long-term situation. Too bad for Clara Cooper, but Addie would still try to find a way to make the trip enjoyable for her too. Even a bit of flirtation might be enough.

CHAPTER THREE

Clara's thoughts kept returning to Miss Barnes as she unpacked first Aunt Matilda's and then her own things. Miss Barnes wasn't much older than her, perhaps a few years at most, but she had an easy grace that Clara couldn't hope to match in a million years. Not to mention her trim figure and perfectly coiffed blond hair, her bright blue eyes that had bored into Clara's so intently.

Could Miss Barnes be somewhere in the bowels of the ship thinking of her right now? Surely, she was being utterly ridiculous. It was part of Miss Barnes's job to make each passenger feel special. Even so, the thought caused a little flutter in her stomach. She had no idea why she was responding this way, like a blushing schoolgirl with her first beau. Perhaps spending this long in close proximity to Aunt Matilda had addled her brain.

Back at home, she seldom saw Aunt Matilda more than a few times a year, which suited her perfectly. Despite living less than twenty miles away, Aunt Matilda and Uncle Henry's life in their Beacon Hill mansion was worlds different from Clara and her family's. The two families were usually content to socialize only at holidays, and Clara knew she had not been Aunt Matilda's first choice for a travel companion. Her uncle's untimely death last year was the only reason she was here now. She'd never spent this much time with her aunt before without the buffer of her mother to take some of the brunt of Matilda's forceful personality, and she wasn't fond of the experience.

She had greatly enjoyed their time in England, marred only by Aunt Matilda's nonstop complaints. Yes, Aunt Matilda had traveled far more than Clara had, but why could she not appreciate the wonders of what they were seeing rather than focusing on all the ways in which it differed from America? The river cruise was the part of the voyage Clara had been most excited for, and she was not going to let Aunt Matilda ruin the experience for her.

As soon as she finished unpacking, she went up to the observation deck. She leaned on the railing, watching Lake Geneva slowly fade from sight as the boat moved up the canal that led to the Rhône that would deposit them in southern France two weeks later. She'd brought her sketchbook, but she left it closed. She wanted to take in the scene rather than try to draw it for later. After a few minutes, she felt someone come stand beside her.

"It's a beautiful view, isn't it? It always makes me a little sad to leave the lake behind," the newcomer said.

Clara turned her head and felt a small thrill when she saw it was Miss Barnes. "I'm rather looking forward to this part of the trip," Clara replied. "A new city every day."

Miss Barnes's smile was dazzling. "Yes, that part is quite exciting. Is this your first time in Europe?"

Clara nodded. "We were in England first, then came here to Switzerland. We'll take the train back up to Paris, and then we'll sail home from Le Havre. I don't know that the route quite makes sense, but it's ever so thrilling."

She started describing how magical their visit to Westminster Abbey had been. Miss Barnes nodded along, but Clara forced herself to stop before she could go on and on and further reveal how unworldly and unsophisticated she was. She decided to turn the focus of the conversation away from herself.

"How long have you been making this trip?"

"I've been on this boat for about eight months. This is my seventh trip going north to south," Miss Barnes said. "We run the same trip in reverse, you see, so I've also done south to north seven times already. Before that, I lived in Paris for several years."

"My goodness, how lovely." It sounded like an ideal life, making one's own living and traveling up and down the river to exotic ports of call. It certainly appealed more than the future that awaited her back in Massachusetts.

Miss Barnes smiled. The boat was picking up speed now, and they could barely see the port anymore. They were leaving Geneva behind, the rolling Swiss countryside flanking them on both sides of the river as they steamed along. "At a certain point, you get a little inured to it all. The sights stay the same, most of the passengers are of the same type… except every so often, when someone more interesting comes along."

She glanced sideways at Clara and back out at the canal. Clara wondered what that meant. Surely, Miss Barnes couldn't be referring to her. Clara had spent so much of her life trying not to attract attention that perhaps she was overly sensitive. Her height had made her the target of schoolyard bullies as a child, and even once she'd finished school and escaped the cruel taunts, she'd never felt comfortable in her body. She slouched as often as she could without her mother or Aunt Matilda scolding her.

Now, though, she felt differently. There was something about the way Miss Barnes looked at her that made her *want* to be noticed. Still, she didn't think there could possibly be anything about her that would cause someone as worldly and well-traveled as Miss Barnes to take an interest in her.

"The joy you are getting from your travels is contagious," Miss Barnes said as if she had read Clara's mind. "One forgets how remarkable it is to see the world…most of the passengers don't have your enthusiasm. It's refreshing."

Heat rose to Clara's cheeks. Her lack of travel experience was something she had been embarrassed about, but here was Miss Barnes acting as if it was a positive attribute.

"I'm glad," she said quietly, not quite able to meet Miss Barnes's gaze.

"I'm afraid I must see to the other passengers now, or they'll be getting jealous. I do hope we'll have the opportunity to speak again soon," Miss Barnes said, a touch of genuine regret in her voice. "Perhaps you'd be willing to show me your drawings sometime?"

"Oh, they're not much to look at. Just doodles, really," Clara muttered. As proud as she'd been of some of them at the time, the thought of Miss Barnes examining them made her second-guess every pencil stroke. She'd sooner show Miss Barnes her diary. It felt less exposing than her art, which often felt like the only way she could fully express herself.

"I'm sure that's nonsense," Miss Barnes said briskly. "In my experience, the best artists are the most self-deprecating. Do enjoy your evening, Miss Cooper." She departed, faint traces of her gardenia and bergamot perfume lingering on the air.

❖

Addie circulated through the dining room in a well-practiced routine, speaking to every guest but never stopping too long at any table. Miss Windermere held court at her table, airily waving her cigarette holder around as she spoke animatedly. She cast several lingering glances at Addie, winking whenever Addie came near.

She could feel Clara's eyes on her throughout dinner, although Clara hurriedly looked away whenever their eyes met. Addie deliberately waited until dinner was nearly over before drifting over to the Coopers' table. Clara seemed shy and unused to so much positive attention, and Addie didn't want to spook her by coming on too strong.

Matilda had waylaid the unfortunate Applebys, a pair of newlyweds, into sitting with them for the meal, and was monologuing at great volume about her late husband. "The late Mr. Cooper Senior was so fond of my Henry, of course," she said. "Why, after Junior died last year, he practically wasted away. If it wasn't for my son, Harry, he probably would have gone even sooner."

"Grandfather already had terminal cancer at that point, didn't he?" Clara asked innocently.

Addie bit back a smile as Matilda paused, clearly annoyed at the interruption of her narrative. She quickly regained her equanimity and continued. "Now Daniel, on the other hand, was always a bit of a black sheep. I hope you don't mind my saying so, Clara dear. I know he's your father, but I find that no good comes of withholding the honest truth. He thought Daniel's ambition to become an artist *quite* unsuitable, and I must say, I agree with him."

Must you really? Addie noted that Clara started slumping her shoulders protectively as soon as Matilda started criticizing her father.

"He still needn't have cut Father off entirely," Clara said, which Addie thought rather brave.

Matilda bristled. "It was his money to do with as he pleased, and he decided Harry was the most deserving recipient. Besides, his attorney says you're in the will as well. He must have left you a small legacy. A very generous thing to do, considering he wasn't on speaking terms with your father. Once the will is through probate and we've heard what it says, you'll see what a truly great man he was. He might have left you enough for a lovely new dress, or perhaps you could even have your hair done properly at last."

The Applebys glanced at each other in mute horror as Clara reddened and stared at her empty plate. Addie felt a swell of vicarious outrage at Matilda's odious behavior and swooped in.

"If you've all finished eating, may I suggest a visit to the passengers' lounge?" she said brightly. "Mrs. Cooper, I suspect the latest issue of *Reader's Digest* will strike your fancy. Mr. Appleby, we have some fine cigars that some of the other gentlemen are already sampling. And perhaps the young ladies would care to see our telescope?"

The group rose from the table, Clara shooting Addie a grateful glance. After depositing Matilda and Mr. Appleby in the lounge, Addie led Clara and Mrs. Appleby toward the observation deck where the little telescope was now set up so the guests could admire the night sky.

Before they could reach it, Mrs. Appleby paused. "You know, I'm rather tired. Thank you very much, Miss Barnes, but I think I'll turn in. Do let my husband know where I've gone if you see him." She gave an exaggerated fake yawn and scurried away.

"That was rather sudden," Clara said, watching her go. "I hope she wasn't embarrassed to be around me after my aunt…"

Addie chuckled. "Oh, I very much doubt it had anything to do with you. I'd bet anything that Mr. Appleby will smoke that cigar in record time. Don't be surprised if the boat starts rocking, even though we're on a river and not an ocean."

"Whatever do you mean?" Clara asked curiously. "Why would the boat—*oh*."

"We've had honeymooners before, and they always follow the same pattern," Addie said, smiling gently so Clara wouldn't think she was laughing at her naivety. "Would you like to look through the telescope now?" She double-checked that the lens was properly focused, then stepped aside so Clara could look. The villages they were drifting past were tiny, so there was nothing to dim the twinkling of thousands of tiny stars.

"They're so beautiful," Clara said, sounding awestruck.

"You live near Boston, yes? I'm sure you can't see nearly this many stars at home."

Clara shook her head. "No. My brother Albert always wanted a telescope when we were growing up, but Mother and Father couldn't aff—well, he never got one. But as you say, he wouldn't have been able to see anything as lovely as this. Where are you from, Miss Barnes?"

"Chicago." She felt eyes on her back and turned to see Hester Windermere watching them from the doorway of the observation deck. Miss Windermere tapped her watch, then jerked her head slightly in the direction of the guest staterooms before slipping away.

Clara, still absorbed in the telescope, had seemingly missed the brief interaction.

"I'm afraid I have some things to attend to before the end of the night, so I'll have to leave you now," Addie said.

Clara looked up, sounding crestfallen. "Oh no. I'm sorry I've been keeping you from your work. It's just been…very nice to speak with you."

Even in the dark, Addie could see the way Clara's cheeks had colored. She injected a touch of regret into her voice as she said, "For me too. I do hope you enjoy the evening. Feel free to stay out here as long as you like."

❖

Addie glanced around the deck to make sure she was unobserved before tapping softly on Miss Windermere's door.

"Come in," Miss Windermere drawled. She was sprawled out on the bed in blush pink satin pajamas, a champagne glass in hand and a lipstick-smeared cigarette dangling from her lips.

"Thank the gods you're here at last. You've been an age. I was about to die of boredom."

Addie laughed and helped herself to champagne. She didn't need to see the label to know that it was the finest variety they had on board. The bubbles exploded on her tongue, the taste smooth and silky as she swallowed the sip. "Would you like some more, Miss Windermere?"

"You calling me 'Miss Windermere' makes me feel about a hundred and ten. It's Hester, darling, at least when we're alone. Please, sit, and let's get to know each other."

Addie topped off Hester's proffered glass and sat in the chair at the dressing table, a nod toward the pretense of propriety. She mustn't appear too eager and cause Hester to think she was only fit for a casual fling.

They chatted for half an hour or so, never letting their glasses get empty. The champagne might have helped, but Addie rather thought she was at her most charming. At any rate, Hester chuckled appreciatively at all of her jokes, her eyes lingering longer and longer on Addie as they finished off the bottle.

"Why don't you come sit by me?" Hester suggested, patting the coverlet beside her. "You're so very far away all over there."

Addie hesitated, feigning indecision. "It's getting awfully late. I'll be in terrible trouble with Captain Vigo if I'm not up before the first passenger in the morning."

Hester exhaled a cloud of cigarette smoke dismissively. "Don't you worry about *him*. With what I'm paying, it's in his best interest to keep me happy."

"Well, all right," Addie said with a giggle. "But I really can't stay too long."

Hester's gaze was positively wolfish as Addie sat on the bed next to her, the mattress dipping slightly from the added weight.

"What a terrible bore, but I suppose I oughtn't keep you up too late. Tonight, at least," Hester said, leaning toward her.

By the time Addie crept back to her own quarters a short while later, her hair was a wreck, and her lipstick completely smudged off. She had kept Hester's wandering hands mostly at bay, but many more evenings like that, and Hester would get bored. It was a delicate balancing act, but she was up for the challenge. The potential reward was worth it.

❖

"What are you doing out here all alone? Come along inside, it's not seemly."

Clara started, not having heard Aunt Matilda approach. She'd been watching Hester Windermere's door, but Miss Barnes hadn't reemerged. She wondered what they could possibly be doing in there for all this time.

"Come along," Aunt Matilda said again, impatiently grabbing Clara's arm. "You young girls may not care about things like your reputation, but any man you'd want to marry certainly will. I take my duty as chaperone very seriously. What happened to Mrs. Appleby and Miss Barnes?"

"Mrs. Appleby went to bed, and Miss Barnes had...work to do," Clara said, glancing again toward the suite on the deck above.

"Well, she oughtn't to have left you here alone," Aunt Matilda chided.

A wave of impatience rose in Clara's chest. Not that she wanted to be attacked or in danger, of course, but she was so desperate for something exciting to happen that she felt quite melancholy that her time on the observation deck had, in fact, been perfectly safe.

"We're not on shore, no one can sneak onto the boat. What do you think could have happened to me?"

"*Tuh.* You're far too naive, my dear," Aunt Matilda said condescendingly, leading the way toward the deck with their staterooms. "Most of the gentlemen passengers seem a decent sort, I'll grant you that, but there's still the crew to think of, and they're almost all *Frenchmen.*"

She peered around suspiciously, as if expecting them to swarm down upon Clara en masse.

"They've all been perfectly polite so far," Clara said. "And Miss Barnes seems like she'd be good at keeping them in line."

Aunt Matilda nodded. "Yes, I quite like what I've seen of that young woman. Such a shame that she has to work, poor thing, but she's making the best of it. Probably hoping she'll meet a wealthy man aboard who'll whisk her away and shower her with furs and jewels."

Clara's mind recoiled at the thought of Miss Barnes being pawed at by some rich old widower as Aunt Matilda continued, "My Harry could see through such schemes, of course, but it's a good thing your brothers aren't traveling with us. They aren't nearly so worldly. Not that they have any fortunes of their own to interest a gold digger."

They had reached the doors of their neighboring staterooms, sparing her from answering. She bade Aunt Matilda a distracted good night and retreated to the safety of her own cabin.

Sleep evaded her, her thoughts buzzing. Normally, she tried to avoid talking to new people, but today, she'd had two conversations with Miss Barnes in which she hadn't embarrassed herself too badly. With any luck, she could keep that up tomorrow.

Chapter Four

The gentle motion of the boat and the chugging steam engines eventually lulled Clara to sleep, and by the time she awoke, they were almost in Lyon. She went out onto the observation deck just in time to see the river widen dramatically as they entered the city. It was so pretty that she almost didn't want to go to breakfast, but her stomach was growling, and she knew she'd be exploring the city up close soon, so she forced herself to go inside.

Moments after she joined Aunt Matilda in the dining room, Hester Windermere slid gracefully into the seat opposite her. "Nice day, isn't it?" she said imperiously, helping herself to the last piece of toast before Clara could take it.

"It is indeed," Aunt Matilda agreed. "I am so looking forward to seeing a bit of Lyon today. I haven't spent much time here before, but I've heard it's lovely."

"It's rather like Paris, except smaller and more provincial," Miss Windermere said, now examining her fingernails.

Undaunted, Aunt Matilda opened the brochure and rattled off the various stops their guided tour would make throughout the day while Miss Windermere watched, an expression of wry amusement on her face.

Clara's reaction was so unexpected that it took her a moment to realize she was feeling defensive of her aunt. It was all well and good for *her* to find fault with Aunt Matilda, but Hester Windermere had no right to look at her with such condescension.

"What brings you on this trip, since you're so familiar with the area already?" Clara asked. Miss Windermere's dark eyes snapped to hers, and Clara willed herself not to flinch. Whatever else Clara might think of her, she had a commanding presence.

"I had some time to kill in between my holiday on the Riviera and my sister's wedding in Paris. I wasn't so sure there would be enough to interest me, but the ship does present certain, ah, diversions."

Miss Windermere was looking past Clara now at Miss Barnes, who had come up behind her to place another rack of toast on the table. Miss Barnes's cheeks were flushed pink, and Clara wondered if she'd just come in from outside or if she was wearing rouge.

"Good morning, ladies. I see you all signed up for the excursion today. We'll depart in fifteen minutes," Miss Barnes said, looking around the table at each of them in turn.

Clara smiled at her warmly when their eyes met, but Miss Barnes only returned it with the neutral half-smile she gave all the passengers. Clara had hoped the conversations they'd shared last night had meant something to Miss Barnes too, but evidently, that wasn't the case. She chastised herself for feeling disappointed by it.

"Do you have a light, Miss Barnes?" Miss Windermere asked.

Silently, Miss Barnes walked over to her and pulled a lighter out of her pocket. As she flicked it open, Miss Windermere grasped her wrist and pulled it close to light her cigarette. Her red nails and stark white fingers contrasted with Miss Barnes's more tanned skin, and she seemed reluctant to let go, even when the tip of her cigarette was glowing. At last, she released Miss Barnes's arm, caressing the back of her hand as she let go.

Miss Barnes pressed her lips together and avoided Clara's eyes as she hurried away. Miss Windermere, on the other hand, gave Clara a hard, steady look as if daring her to say something. Aunt Matilda was still engrossed in the brochure, so Clara couldn't gauge her reaction.

Clara looked away, her cheeks warm and probably flushed. Blood pounded in her ears, and she would have liked nothing more than to tell Miss Windermere to keep her hands to herself and to leave Miss Barnes alone. Her brain refused to form the words, which was probably a blessing in disguise. She had no indication that Miss Barnes was unhappy with what had happened. It was only Clara who was upset by it, for some unknown reason.

❖

Once the walking tour of Lyon commenced, Clara was too busy admiring the beauty around her to focus on anything else. The winding cobblestone streets led past row upon row of charming stone houses, restaurants, and patisseries. She heard smatterings of French from passersby. It had been a while since her high school French classes, but she understood a few words here and there.

They visited the remains of a Roman amphitheater, explored the charming streets of Old Lyon, and sampled a variety of delicious cheeses at a fromagerie. Even with only Aunt Matilda for company, Clara was captivated by the beauty all around her.

Every time she looked for Miss Barnes, she was with Miss Windermere at the back of the group, looking engrossed in whatever she was saying. Clara felt a flash of jealousy, wishing she was the one keeping Miss Barnes so entertained. She would have much rather been talking to Miss Barnes instead of Aunt Matilda, who was ignoring all the sights around them in favor of complaining about the roughness of the cobblestones on her shoes.

Their last stop before returning to the ship was the Basilica of Notre Dame de Fourvière. Clara craned her neck to look at the ornate mosaics on the ceiling while the guide described the history and construction of the cathedral. Everywhere she turned, there was still more beautiful art. Stained glass windows, more tiled mosaic murals, and elaborately carved statues adorned the huge space.

Aunt Matilda was muttering imprecations about idolatrous Catholic art, but Clara tuned her out as she admired the murals. She wandered away from the group, lost in awe at how much work and craftsmanship had gone into creating such a magnificent place. She tried to soak in all the details she could to tell her father about when she got home. He would appreciate it as much as she did.

The guide pointed out the staircase that led to the only one of the four tall towers that was open to the public. Aunt Matilda was loath to part with the extra ten francs it cost for admission to the tower, but she begrudgingly allowed Clara to go up on her own.

Hardly anyone from the group wanted to go into the tower, so Clara found herself ascending the stairs alone between an Italian family and a group of French nuns. It was a long climb up to the rooftop, but the view was well worth it when she got there. She stood against the railing trying to catch her breath, a trickle of sweat running down her back.

Of course, after being unavailable all day, Miss Barnes chose that moment to come stand beside her. Clara dabbed at her face with her handkerchief, sure she was flushed and shiny with exertion. She hadn't realized Miss Barnes was also climbing up; she must have been shielded from view by the nuns.

"What do you think of the view?" Miss Barnes asked, gesturing out at the city.

An endless array of red-tiled roofs spread below them, dotted by little parks and green spaces. The smaller Saone River, flowing in to join the Rhône, glittered here and there between the buildings.

"It's beautiful," Clara said. "Won't Miss Windermere be looking for you?"

"She said she doesn't have a head for heights and was staying on the ground," Miss Barnes said. "Besides, she's just one passenger among many. She doesn't get to demand all my time. When I saw you heading up here by yourself, I thought I'd take advantage of it."

Clara was flattered that after spending all day with Miss Windermere, Miss Barnes had deliberately sought her out. She leaned forward on the railing. "That's too bad, being afraid of heights. I love it up here. I can almost imagine being a bird, soaring around up above, able to see everything looking tiny down below."

"Careful there, or you'll find out if you can really fly," Miss Barnes said, laughing. She leaned against the railing, her face turning pensive. "I think I know what you mean. It makes our troubles seem insignificant somehow, doesn't it?"

Miss Barnes's tone made Clara think she was talking about something specific. "What are your troubles?" she asked curiously.

Miss Barnes swallowed hard as she looked out at the city, and Clara hoped she hadn't overstepped. "I lost someone close to me, a very dear…friend. Last year."

"I'm so sorry." Impulsively, Clara reached out and touched the back of Miss Barnes's hand where it gripped the railing. She regretted it immediately, remembering Miss Windermere clutching at Miss Barnes at the breakfast table, but before she could drop her hand, Miss Barnes grasped it with her own.

"Thank you," she said, squeezing. "It's been very hard, and I can't really talk about it with anyone. I shouldn't be burdening you with it, either. I don't even know why I am. I'm sorry."

"Don't be sorry. I don't mind, really. Tell me about your friend."

"Her name was Eva. She was from Switzerland. We met in Chicago, and then we lived together in Paris. She was funny and smart and beautiful, and the most…most *alive* person I ever knew."

Clara could hear the pain in her voice. She couldn't imagine enduring such a devastating loss, especially with her family thousands of miles away. She wished there was something she could do to comfort Miss Barnes, but she didn't know what would help.

Before she could think of something, she heard approaching voices on the stairs.

Miss Barnes released her hurriedly. "I'm very sorry to have taken up your time. I'd appreciate it if you didn't mention this to the captain. I'm not supposed to share personal information with the passengers. Make sure you're back at the boat by seven o'clock tonight."

Before Clara could say anything else, Miss Barnes slipped away and vanished down the stairs.

❖

It had been foolish of Addie to open up so much about Eva to Clara Cooper. Idiotic, really. Clara herself was unlikely to cause any problems with the captain or with Hester, but if she told her aunt, and the wretched woman read between the lines…

Well, that was a bridge she'd cross if it came to it, but she needn't have gone borrowing trouble.

No good could come of baring her soul to someone like Clara. Even if Clara's naivety didn't lead her to inadvertently expose Addie, it was risky to give someone so much power over her. It would probably be best to avoid her for the rest of the trip, at least any time alone with her.

The idea made her unexpectedly sad. She had been so lonely since Eva had died that one year had felt like decades. Clara was so different from the passengers Addie usually met on the ship, idealistic and empathetic. Addie sensed an innate kindness from Clara that she wished she deserved. She wished she could confide in her fully enough to confess that as heartbroken as she was by Eva's death, she also bore some resentment at Eva leaving her penniless to fend for herself.

If she was completely honest, she had to admit that Clara's attention was flattering too. She had sensed Clara's eyes seeking her out all day and had jumped at the chance to escape from Hester's clutches long enough to fuel the attraction. She hadn't expected to reveal as much as she had.

She crept along the deck to Hester's suite again that night, still pondering what to do about Clara. Staying away was the smart decision. She had been on the verge of telling her all about Eva, for goodness' sake; information like that could ruin her, no matter how good-hearted Clara was.

Once she was with Hester, her mind was fully occupied with keeping up the persona she'd adopted. She smiled at all the right moments, sometimes coyly and other times more lasciviously, told jokes that made Hester's eyes light up with glee, and tossed back champagne like it was water. It was a relief to rid her mind of worry over Clara and the mess of guilt and sadness she felt about Eva, if only for a few hours.

"However shall we keep ourselves entertained tonight?" Hester asked, slowly shoving Addie's skirt up to reveal her stocking-clad thigh.

"Not that." Addie pushed Hester's hand away and tugged her skirt back down demurely.

Hester pouted. "And I thought you were up for a good time."

"I'm no prude, but you've got to try harder than that," Addie said, fluttering her lashes. She had a hunch that she'd do better to hold off Hester for another night or two, lest she be too easy a conquest. Hester seemed like the type of woman who only wanted something she had to work for. She'd never had to play these sorts of mind games with Eva; their relationship had unfolded naturally. Eva's fortune had set them apart, but in all other ways, they had been equals.

"How fond would you say you are of this job?" Hester asked conversationally.

Addie kept her face as neutral as she could while she considered the question. She thought she knew why Hester was asking, and how she answered might shape her entire future. "Reasonably well, I suppose. It's not what I dreamed of doing, but no one gets to live their dreams, do they?"

"I do," Hester said matter-of-factly. "When I want something, I simply buy it."

"Not everything's for sale."

Hester gave her a pitying look. "Of course it is, my dear girl. It's only a matter of finding the right price. I'm not speaking only of money. Sometimes, there are other currencies. Security, for instance, or an invitation to join a particular club or attend an exclusive event."

Security. Hester had hit upon Addie's strongest desire at the first try. If she had even a tenth of Hester's wealth, she would never have to worry a day in her life. There would never be a question of where her next meal was coming from or if she would have somewhere safe to sleep that night. If she played her cards right with Hester, she could be setting herself up for a very comfortable life indeed.

CHAPTER FIVE

Over the next few days, Clara stayed close to Miss Barnes and Miss Windermere on the excursions ashore. Usually, they were joined at the hip, but every so often, Miss Barnes wriggled free and spent time with the other guests. Try as Clara might, however, she didn't end up alone with Miss Barnes again.

She thought to befriend some of the other passengers instead, but most of them were her aunt's age or older, not to mention extremely wealthy, and she had little in common with them. Mrs. Appleby was younger and more fun to talk to, but she and her new husband seldom left the boat, and when they did, they went off alone. Clara wished she could tag along, but she remembered what Miss Barnes had said about newlyweds and gave them a wide berth.

Instead, she mostly kept to herself, taking in the sights and devouring whatever her guidebook had to say about the area. She remembered her father reminiscing about the grand tour of Europe he and his friends had taken after college and how wistful he was not to be able to provide the same experience for his own children.

Her two brothers had made it to Europe anyway, but serving in the Great War was hardly comparable. They were lucky to have made it home physically unscathed, and she knew they both suffered from nightmares. Part of her wished she could go to the battle sites in northern France where they had fought, but the more cowardly side was relieved to remain far away.

Neither Fred nor Albie would tell her much about their time on the front, changing the subject if she brought it up. As much as she wanted to understand what they had endured and to see the battlefields, she had to admit, she was afraid to. She had read too much about the horrors of the trenches and no-man's-land to want to see it for herself.

She was so busy feeling ashamed of her own cowardice that she scarcely took in a word of the guide's speech in the castle they were touring.

"Rather dull, all these castles, aren't they? They do blend together after a while."

Clara jumped slightly. The faded silk carpets on the floor had masked the sound of Hester Windermere's chic heels clicking as she approached.

"I suppose so," she stammered. There was a harsh coldness to Miss Windermere's manner that she found off-putting. It always felt like the woman was secretly laughing at her.

"Then again, you Americans are rather easily charmed. Especially those from more provincial places."

Miss Windermere gave an airy chuckle that made the hairs on the back of Clara's neck rise. Although her expensive wardrobe and aristocratic bearing set her apart from anyone Clara knew back home, that laugh and the smile that didn't reach Miss Windermere's eyes exposed her for what she was: a bully.

"I think my aunt is looking for me," Clara said, beating a hasty retreat.

She avoided Miss Windermere after that. She had spent too much time in her life being the butt of others' jokes to subject herself to it while she was supposed to be enjoying herself on vacation.

Fortunately, there was plenty to distract Clara from her non-ideal travel companions. As the boat wound its way farther south along the Rhône, every day brought new sights and wonders.

Outside the city of Valence, they visited the ruins of a twelfth-century castle near the summit of a mountain. After exploring the ruins thoroughly, Clara hiked up the mountain a little farther so she could draw it from a distance. As she opened her sketchbook, she wondered what the castle's original inhabitants would have made of the modern world. They hadn't even known of the existence of the Americas, while she was able to travel across the ocean on a simple six-day steamship voyage.

On the way back to the boat in Valence, Clara was tempted by the delicious scents of spiced lamb and freshly baked bread wafting out of the city's Armenian district, but Aunt Matilda gave her a look of such horror when she suggested it that she dropped the idea.

"This French food is difficult enough for my digestion," Aunt Matilda said. "I won't upset it further with...*foreign* cuisine."

Clara longed to point out that French food was also foreign to them, but she didn't think Aunt Matilda would appreciate that distinction. Instead, she kept her face blank and made a mental note to tell her brothers about it in her next letter home.

With the time it took for transatlantic mail to be delivered, she might well be home by the time the letters arrived, but she sent them off every few days anyway. It guaranteed she wouldn't forget anything she wanted to share with her family, and it was safer than keeping a diary that Aunt Matilda might read.

Back on the boat, she folded up her sketch of the castle and put it in the envelope with her letter detailing the day's events, then dropped it off in the communications office to be posted at the next port of call. She thought the drawing was rather good for something she had done so quickly, but she wasn't so attached to it that she'd be devastated if it got lost in the mail. It was a nice change to be proud of her art, and she hoped her family would be too. Even if nothing momentous came of the trip, at least she had something to show for it.

Chapter Six

Addie felt like she was trying to balance on a tightrope, keeping Hester charmed and entertained while also not neglecting Clara. She couldn't help but feel Clara was getting short shrift, but Hester was proving to be demanding. No matter how much Addie might prefer Clara's company, Hester was too promising a prospect to ignore.

She was pleased that Clara was keeping her distance from Hester. Hester had an acerbic tongue and a sense of humor that frequently verged on cruelty. The last thing Addie wanted was her focusing on Clara.

Much to her chagrin, Hester raised the subject one night as they shared a postcoital cigarette. "I cannot abide that dreadful Cooper creature," Hester said, exhaling smoke through her nostrils.

Addie snorted derisively. "She's a real piece of work, isn't she? I try to escape her as quickly as possible, but it's hard to get a word in edgewise."

"Not the old bag," Hester said dismissively. "Well, her too. I meant the girl. There's something rather pitiful about her, don't you think?"

Addie fell still beside her. Who in their right mind would have more objection to Clara than to Matilda?

Hester continued without waiting for an answer. "If there's one thing I simply cannot stand, it's timidity. At least the old lady has the guts to be herself, to demand attention. That girl is always skulking about, cringing whenever one tries to talk to her. She follows you around like a lovesick puppy."

Addie gripped a handful of bedsheet, trying to maintain her composure. Hadn't she had similar thoughts herself, even deliberately encouraged Clara with attention and flattery? It all sounded much crueler coming from Hester's mouth, though. What right had she to say such things about Clara, who was never anything but kind and eager for just a little kindness in return?

Hester propped herself up on an elbow, turning to look at Addie. "Oh, come now. Surely, you must have noticed? You can barely take a step without tripping over her."

Addie struggled to keep her tone neutral. "I think she's...very lonely, with only her awful aunt for company. Given that, it's natural that she should be drawn to me. After all, it's my job to ensure that all the guests have a nice time."

It was Hester's turn to scoff. "Yes, I'm sure she'd like nothing more than to have a *nice time* with you. The way she looks at you, honestly. It's pathetic."

"Are you jealous?" Addie teased. Her stomach was still twisting with guilt, and she was eager to move the conversation away from Clara's supposed shortcomings.

"Jealous of *that*? Don't be absurd," Hester snipped. "If I thought you'd even consider her for a moment, you wouldn't be worth having."

Something in Addie recoiled at the disdain in Hester's voice. "Maybe you don't know me as well as you think. I could be interested in something a bit different for a change."

Hester's eyes flashed. "Watch yourself, my girl. I don't like to share my things."

Addie shifted uncomfortably. Hester's tone was light, but there was an undercurrent of danger in her expression. Addie didn't at all care for Hester referring to her as a possession, but she didn't dare say so.

What did it matter if Hester was scornful of Clara? It didn't affect Addie in the slightest, and it wasn't as if Clara would ever find out. It was far more important to solidify her position with Hester, which clearly wouldn't be helped by pushing back.

All the same, it didn't feel right to sit and listen to such things. She left as soon as she could, making up an evening errand she needed to attend to before bed. She didn't want to say something in the heat of the moment that she'd regret later.

The next morning, Captain Vigo stopped Addie on her way into the dining room to oversee breakfast. "The elite stateroom will need to be thoroughly cleaned," he said. "Miss Windermere unfortunately must leave us in Montélimar."

Ice flooded Addie's veins. She had laid all the groundwork, and now Hester was leaving early? Outwardly, she kept her cool, but her mind was roiling. She made an excuse to leave the captain as quickly as possible and sped to Hester's cabin where she found the door ajar. Hester's luggage was all neatly packed and ready for travel. Hester herself was dressed in the same suit she'd worn upon arrival, a black beret perched on her head insouciantly.

"You're leaving?"

"Oh yes, didn't I tell you?" Hester said in a bored tone, starting to pull on her gloves. "My idiot sister decided to get married in Paris this Saturday, and I simply must attend. Personally, I think by the time one is on to one's third marriage, one has forfeited the right to a large wedding, don't you? But allowances must be made for the foibles of one's family, I suppose." She didn't even give Addie a passing glance as she checked her reflection in the mirror, making a minute adjustment to her hair.

"But I had hoped..." Addie tried to keep the desperation out of her voice.

Hester sighed in irritation. "Oh, don't make a scene. We're both adults here. I know perfectly well what you hoped, my dear. You think you're the first pretty girl who thought all she had to do is open her legs a few times, and I'd lose my head for her? Hardly."

When Addie was eleven, she had gotten into a fight at school, and Susan Kendrick had punched her in the stomach. She hadn't thought of the incident in years, but now she was right back in that schoolyard, her lungs refusing to take in air, her hands shaking from mingled shock and fury. "You never intended to take me with you," she finally managed to say, forcing her face into an expressionless mask.

"Of course I didn't," Hester said matter-of-factly. "Tell me honestly, if I had told you I only wanted a few nights of fun with no financial benefit to you, would you ever have come here that first night?"

Addie shook her head mutely, acknowledging the truth in Hester's words. Inwardly, she seethed at how thoroughly Hester had out-gamed her. It was humiliating, really.

"Chin up, my girl. I've no doubt that in time, your suitably gullible white whale will come along, and you'll be cunning enough to land *her*," Hester said. Addie wanted to slap the condescension off her smug face, but she managed to restrain herself. "I did enjoy our time together. I'd hate for it to be a complete waste of your effort."

Hester paused in the doorway, opened her pocketbook, and took out a ten pound note. She held it out, but Addie, now quivering with rage, made no move to take it. Hester laughed softly, let the bill flutter to the floor, and left without another word.

Addie let the door slam shut behind her and sank onto the bed. Hester had taken advantage of her, but far worse, she'd made a fool of her. She clenched her fists a few times, but it wasn't enough to dispel her pent-up emotions, so she buried her face in the pillows and screamed. The only saving grace was that no one else knew about her and Hester. That was, no one other than Clara.

She wasn't sure exactly how much Clara had grasped of her relationship with Hester, but she couldn't take the risk. Clara could never know what had happened. Addie had no doubt that she'd be sympathetic, but she didn't want anyone's sympathy, least of all Clara's. The idea of Clara pitying her was intolerable. Somehow, she had to ensure that the balance of power in their relationship stayed the way it was.

She sat up slowly, a scheme already forming in her mind. Hester's description of Clara as a lovesick puppy was cruel but not necessarily inaccurate. If Clara was already that devoted to Addie from just a few smiles and some kind words now and then, how much more would she be if Addie managed to seduce her? After that, Clara would never dream of revealing Addie's humiliation at Hester's hands to anyone else.

Addie had always loved planning, and her frustration at her failure with Hester was already fading as she tucked the note into her pocket and left to go find Clara. The money might have been intended as an insult, but she was far too practical to let it go to waste.

CHAPTER SEVEN

Clara was sitting on the observation deck with her sketchbook, a gentle breeze cutting through the humidity and riffling her hair. A few minutes ago, she and Aunt Matilda had watched Hester Windermere climb into the back of a Rolls-Royce waiting alongside the port. The car had sped away, eventually followed by a small truck loaded with her copious luggage.

"It's a shame she left early. She was a nice, lively presence aboard," Aunt Matilda said.

"She may have been lively, but she certainly wasn't very nice. I'm glad she's gone," Clara said. In fact, she was quite looking forward to the rest of the trip now that Miss Windermere wouldn't be able to keep Miss Barnes busy all the time.

"*Tuh.* How uncharitable you are, Clara," Aunt Matilda said patronizingly. "Miss Windermere is used to a certain standard of living back in England, and it's quite reasonable of her to demand it here too."

Clara considered saying that in that case, perhaps Miss Windermere should never have left England in the first place, but she kept the thought to herself. It wasn't worth the scolding it would doubtlessly earn about respecting her elders and those of Miss Windermere's social standing.

Aunt Matilda rose, wrapping her shawl around herself and shivering dramatically. "It's getting rather chilly out here. Let's go in and start dressing for dinner."

"It's still an hour until dinner. I think I'll stay out here awhile longer," Clara said. The temperature still felt perfectly comfortable to her, having grown up in New England without central heating. More appealing, though, was the opportunity of a few Matilda-free minutes on her own.

"I suppose that's all right, but mind you don't catch a chill," Aunt Matilda said, eyeing her skeptically.

After she left, Clara looked around to confirm that she was alone on the observation deck. *Ah, bliss.*

She relaxed in her deck chair, basking in the sudden quiet. She could hear the gentle thumps of smaller boats bumping into the dock, the hum of insects, and the occasional auto engine and clopping of hooves coming from the streets near the port. She wished she could spend every evening like this, free from anyone's scrutiny or unwanted chatter. She left her sketchbook unopened on her lap, choosing to spend the time daydreaming instead.

She let herself fantasize about the life she would lead if money were no object. Maybe she would have a small apartment in a city somewhere, then a nice sprawling manor out in the country. She would keep a full set of paints and brushes at both properties, of course. No more skimping on restocking her supplies, deciding to paint this flower instead of that one because Father had run out of blue paint and couldn't afford more until his next payday. The little divot between her mother's eyes when she frowned over the household account books, trying to stretch out their food for another week, would never reappear. She could buy her brothers whatever they wanted, even set them up in business so they could afford to get married and start families if they wanted to.

The thought of marriage brought the fantasy crashing down. It was all well and good to go off on ridiculous flights of fancy, but she had to accept that she lived in reality. Once she got back home, she needed to put her mind to making a realistic plan for her future. Maybe if the bequest from her grandfather was large enough, she could afford a shorthand course and become a secretary. It was a far cry from the life of adventure she dreamed of, but at least it was a living that didn't depend on finding a husband.

She heard footsteps on the stairs leading to the observation deck.

"There you are, Miss Cooper. I've been looking for you all over."

Clara's heart leapt at the sound of Miss Barnes's voice. "Well, you've found me."

"I hope you weren't avoiding me," Miss Barnes teased, grinning.

Clara shook her head, hoping she wasn't blushing. She couldn't think of anything witty to say. Or anything at all, really. Now that she knew Miss Windermere wasn't going to come along and drag Miss Barnes away, she felt pressure to be interesting enough to keep her attention.

"Do you mind if I join you? I don't want to intrude if you'd rather be by yourself," Miss Barnes said.

"Not at all. Please do." If it had been anyone else, it would have felt like an intrusion, but instead, there was only a frisson of excitement as Miss Barnes gracefully sank into the chair next to hers.

"I love coming up here when there's no one else around. It's peaceful." Miss Barnes produced knitting needles and yarn from her shoulder bag and started to knit.

"It must be nice for you to get a little break from all the guests wanting things all the time," Clara said.

Miss Barnes nodded, her needles clicking quietly as she spoke. "I'll deny it if you tell anyone I said this, but sometimes, I want to run and hide from all of them."

Clara smiled. Apparently, Miss Barnes didn't lump her in with all the other passengers. "You might have some more free time now that Miss Windermere is gone."

"Oh, *her*," Miss Barnes said disdainfully. "Many of our guests are high maintenance. I don't mind it really. It comes with the job. But she was an entirely different level of demanding, all hours of the day and night…it's a relief to see her go."

"I was thinking the same thing."

Miss Barnes looked around guiltily. "I shouldn't be talking like this. I keep forgetting you're a guest like everyone else. It's very unprofessional. I feel so comfortable with you that I speak too freely."

"I'm glad of it. I'm not like these snobby rich people. I'd much rather we be friends." Clara could barely believe her own nerve at speaking so openly.

"I'd like that too. The captain would frown on it and probably your aunt as well, so we'll have to be a bit circumspect. But since we've got some time before dinner, we can talk for a bit in private."

All the boldness seemed to leave Clara's body, and she couldn't think of a single conversation topic. "What shall we talk about? Do you want to tell me more about Eva?"

Miss Barnes's eyes widened at the mention of her late friend's name, but she shook her head. "No, let's stick to cheerier subjects. What's the first thing you're going to do when you return home?" She turned toward Clara in her chair, her face attentive.

Being the focus of her attention was heady, almost disorienting. It reminded Clara of a few times in high school when she would get so distracted by a particularly pretty classmate talking to her that she'd lose track of the conversation. She looked out over the river instead to keep from getting tongue-tied. "I was thinking about that right before you got here," she said. "It's not the happiest thought for me, I'm afraid. To be honest, I don't have many prospects. I might look into secretarial school."

"What about your art? You seem so passionate about that. Surely, there's a way to turn that into a career?"

Clara laughed dully. She had seen firsthand her father's failed attempts to make it as an artist without money or a wealthy backer. Add being a woman and it was an impossible dream. It was a hobby for the wealthy, not a vocation. "I need to stick to more realistic aspirations."

"I'm sorry to hear that. I suppose it's only the Miss Windermeres and Mrs. Coopers of the world who get to do whatever they want."

"That's too true. What are you making?" Clara asked, gesturing at the knitting.

"A pair of mittens," Miss Barnes said, holding up one completed mitten and the other in progress.

Clara squinted at them. Something about the finished mitten looked off, but she couldn't figure out what it was at first. "Does it have two thumbs?"

Miss Barnes nodded, her fingers once again flying over her needles. "Yes. I bought the wool when Eva and I were in Norway last year. A lot of the fishermen wear these. If the palms get wet while they're out at sea, they can simply flip it over, and it's like having a whole new pair. I thought it was a clever idea, and I wanted to try it for myself."

Clara had never even thought of Norway as a place one could visit. Miss Barnes and her friend must have lived a more exotic life than she could possibly imagine. "Were you working on a riverboat there too?" she asked, for want of anything cleverer to say.

"No, we were tourists. We went on a boat tour of some of the fjords, actually. I suppose having been a passenger on a similar vessel gives me a bit of an advantage now that I work on one. Before I came here, I worked as a lady's companion. For a few different American ladies until I met Eva." Miss Barnes's voice softened with emotion.

"Did you like being a companion?" Clara had heard of ladies' companions before, but no one she knew was in a position to need or afford one. Maybe if Aunt Matilda hadn't had Clara, she would have hired someone to accompany her on this trip instead. Her aunt would be easier to tolerate if she was being paid for it.

"There are good parts of it and bad parts, as with any line of work," Miss Barnes said. "It's easier than being a servant, but you are still at someone else's beck and call. Some of the ladies I've worked for have been very…demanding."

"Like Miss Windermere?" Clara said. Miss Barnes looked at her sharply. "I mean because she was always cornering you and taking up all your time in the evenings."

Miss Barnes visibly relaxed. "Oh, I thought you might mean something else. Yes, she reminded me a lot of some of my previous employers. Eva was never like that, though." She looked out at the river and seemed lost in thought at some private memory.

"Despite our best efforts, we ended up on the same unhappy topics," Clara pointed out.

Miss Barnes smiled at her in a way that made her pulse quicken. "Good point. We might as well delve into your art if we're going to be thorough about it. I'm very curious about it. Would you be willing to show me some of your work?"

"Oh, you don't want to see them," Clara said, horror-struck at the very idea. She poured so much of herself into her drawings. Letting someone else look at them would feel far too personal. Even her father only got to see a carefully curated selection, and he was biased by paternal love.

"I do," Miss Barnes insisted, but Clara shook her head. "Well, I can't force you, of course, but if you change your mind, I'm always happy to look at them. We can talk about other things if you'd prefer. What sort of films do you like?"

Clara was relieved that she'd changed the subject, and they fell into an easy conversation. They had both been thrilled by the transition to talkies and agreed that Greta Garbo was destined to become even more of a star now that her beautiful husky voice could be heard.

"What destination are you most looking forward to?" Miss Barnes asked once their discussion of movies had run its course.

"Arles," Clara replied without hesitation. "Vincent Van Gogh is my favorite painter, and to see the place that inspired some of his greatest works is a dream come true."

"Maybe you'll find similar inspiration there."

"I hope so," Clara said. She certainly wouldn't dream of putting herself in the same class as Van Gogh, but maybe a bit of his spirit would rub off on her. She dearly hoped so. As the trip rolled on, time was running out for the momentous adventure she had been longing for.

CHAPTER EIGHT

Addie smiled at the fervid excitement in Clara's voice when she talked about going to Arles. She couldn't remember the last time she had felt so earnestly enthusiastic about something. Certainly not since Eva's passing.

"I hope you've saved enough room in your sketchbook for all the drawings you'll be inspired to do when we go to Arles," she said to Clara that evening after dinner.

"I'm sure I have. It's not like I'm a real artist." Clara's face darkened and turned wistful.

"You shouldn't be so hard on yourself," Addie insisted. "I'm sure your art is lovely. Do you think you might let me see it now?"

Clara bit her lip, hesitating. "Oh fine, but please don't judge them too harshly." She led the way to her cabin and pulled out her sketchbook. She looked away as Addie flicked it open, apparently not wanting to see her reaction.

Addie's mouth fell open as she looked through it. She forgot all about her plans both to bolster Clara's self-esteem and ensure her silence, transfixed by the sketches. They were unpolished, and some were smeared with eraser marks, but Clara had a natural eye and an innate talent. The first few pages were filled with scenes of London, then gradually transitioned to the more familiar sights along the boat's itinerary.

"They're beautiful," she whispered, ghosting her hand over an outline that she recognized as the Palais des Papes in Avignon.

"You don't need to lie. They're mediocre just like me, and that's all I'll ever be. You've heard enough from Aunt Matilda. You know it's true. I'm too big, and I have poor posture, and my hair is ugly, and no man will ever want to marry me. Clumsy Clara, that's what the other girls used to call me in school. Better than Clara the Cow, which is what some of the boys called me. They used to *moo* when I walked by."

Clara's lip trembled, and a few tears trickled out of the corners of her eyes. Addie stared at her, shocked by the outburst. She would have dearly loved to hop into Mr. Wells's time machine and give Clara's bullies a swift kick in the pants. Perhaps Matilda Cooper could "accidentally" fall overboard; that might be some comfort. No wonder Clara so often hunched over, trying to make herself look smaller.

Clara avoided her gaze, and Addie spoke quietly as if trying to calm a spooked animal. "I'm not lying. I really do think your art is beautiful. And so are you."

"*Tuh,*" Clara said, a perfect imitation of her aunt. She gave a watery smile. "That's very kind of you to say."

"I can tell you don't believe me, but perhaps in time, I'll be able to convince you," Addie said sternly. She cupped Clara's cheek.

Clara's eyes fluttered shut, and she inhaled sharply. "I realize I don't even know your first name," she whispered.

"Adeline. Addie," Addie said, batting her eyelashes ever so slightly.

"Addie," Clara repeated, and Addie moved in close.

Miss Barnes—Addie—pulled back before their lips could touch. "Miss Cooper, I'm sorry—"

"Won't you please call me Clara?" Clara interrupted.

Addie bit her lip, and Clara couldn't stop staring at her mouth. "I should go," she said finally, turning toward the door.

"Wait!" Clara said desperately. "I…I want you to stay."

Addie stopped with her hand on the knob. She stood stock still, then slowly turned back to face her. Her heart thumped in her throat as Addie looked at her, blue eyes blazing.

Addie's attention was intoxicating, as powerful as the little sips of moonshine her brothers sometimes let her steal. When Addie called her beautiful, she wanted to believe it, perhaps even *did* believe it for a moment. She seized every ounce of courage she had and swooped down to kiss Addie's lips.

After a pause that felt like a lifetime, Addie was kissing her back. Her touch was feverish, devouring, and Clara melted onto the bed. Addie lowered herself on top of her, her warm weight sending sparks of pleasure through Clara's body.

"Oh, Addie," she moaned, and Addie clapped a hand over her mouth.

"You have to be quiet," she hissed. "I could get in so much trouble."

Clara nodded contritely, and Addie removed her hand with a warning glance. Clara bit back another moan as Addie kissed her again, her body flooding with sensation. As Addie trailed kisses down her neck, Clara wrapped her arms around her, caressing her back.

Eagerly, she helped Addie shove her skirt up. When Addie's hand wandered inside her drawers and started stroking her, her hips nearly bucked up off the bed.

"That feels...*oh*..." She trailed off, clenching her teeth to keep from crying out.

She'd woken up sometimes in the night from a lurid dream with her hand up under the skirt of her nightgown, but she'd never felt anything like this before. White hot bolts of pleasure shot through her as Addie caressed her hot folds with deft fingers. Addie brushed against a spot Clara had felt before, a little bump that caused waves of almost overwhelming sensation and made her whimper quietly.

"Oh, you like *that*," Addie whispered, smiling down at her wickedly.

She kept rubbing at the magic spot, and Clara had to bite her hand to muffle the noises coming out of her mouth. Moments later, she was flying off a cliff as a wave of ecstasy washed over her. Addie kept touching her through it, only trailing off when Clara flinched from overstimulation.

She caught Addie's eye and grinned bashfully, but before she could say anything, the door handle started rattling. They both leapt to their feet and away from each other, Clara hurriedly smoothing down her dress as Aunt Matilda came into her stateroom.

"Clara, are you hiding in here? Honestly, I—oh, hello, Miss

Barnes," Aunt Matilda boomed. "This door is sticking. It just won't do. It won't do at all. What if there was a fire?"

"We're on a boat surrounded by water. I could always jump out the window," Clara said, and she was gratified to see Addie turn away so her aunt wouldn't see her smile.

"I'll have the handyman come and look at it right away," Addie said, having regained her composure. "I do apologize, Mrs. Cooper."

"*Tuh*," Aunt Matilda said skeptically, then turned her eagle eye back to her niece. "Clara, the Brodericks have invited us to play bridge with them tomorrow night, isn't that nice? It'll be good for you to get to know them before their son comes aboard in a few days. He's thirty-eight and not yet married, you know."

A mantle of dread settled onto Clara's shoulders. An evening playing a boring game with boring people, all to prepare herself to be shoved at another young man her well-intentioned but clueless family was hoping she'd marry. The experience would be nothing but awkward for both her and the Brodericks' unfortunate son.

It was hard to believe that mere minutes ago, she'd been in the throes of the greatest pleasure she'd ever experienced. Addie looked as cool and unruffled as ever, not a hair on her golden head out of place. No one would ever look at her and guess what had happened between them.

"Good night, Mrs. Cooper, Miss Cooper. I'll see you in the morning," Addie said. She gave them both the same neutral smile from their arrival and swept out of the room without looking back.

The next morning, Clara entered the dining room with mingled excitement and trepidation. Her heart jumped in her throat when she saw Addie floating gracefully around the room, saying good morning to each guest and dropping off brochures about the excursions at the next port of call.

She had no idea how to act around Addie after what had happened between them the night before. She was so attuned to Addie's presence that she managed to completely ignore Aunt Matilda's prattle for a change. Thankfully, her aunt was as oblivious as ever. When Addie finally came over to their table, Clara's pulse shot sky high.

"How did you sleep, Miss Cooper?" Addie asked, her eyes twinkling. "I hope you are enjoying your breakfast."

"I slept very well, thank you," Clara said. Her smile might have been slightly too wide than the situation called for, but she was proud that her voice sounded steady. She took a deep sip from her glass, which turned out to contain a delicious peach nectar.

"The mattress was rather lacking, I'm afraid," Aunt Matilda said. "I admit, I am most particular about them. Why, at home, I change the mattress so often that Henry said we ought to buy stock in the Sealy Corporation. Come to think of it, I may do so once Mr. Cooper Senior's estate is settled."

Clara gritted her teeth. Aunt Matilda, Uncle Henry, and their son had always sucked up to Grandfather to stay in his good graces, knowing how mercurial the old man could be. Although the details of his will hadn't been released yet, he had thoughtfully sent Clara's father a letter that his grandson Harry would inherit his fortune, rather than his disfavored son. Clara supposed she should have been grateful that he had apparently left her something, but she was too resentful of his ill treatment of her beloved father to care very much.

"I would be glad to see about switching out the mattress for you, Mrs. Cooper," Addie said blandly.

Aunt Matilda waved her fork airily. "That won't be necessary, Miss Barnes. I truly doubt there is anything aboard that will be suitable. I shall simply make do. I'm certainly not one to complain. I think I'll take a turn about the deck now to get some air."

Clara and Addie managed to contain their snickers until Aunt Matilda had left the dining room. Addie pressed her hands over her mouth, desperately trying to stop.

"Mademoiselle Barnes, you seem to have found something very amusing," came a deep voice. "I certainly hope it's not at a passenger's expense."

The captain had entered the dining room without either of them noticing, and was now looking at Addie sternly. Immediately, Addie stopped laughing, her expression worried.

Clara jumped in to save her. "Oh no, Captain Vigo. I was recounting a time that a…goat ate my brother's, uh…bicycle…tire?"

"Yes. Yes, that's it," Addie said unconvincingly. "It was more in Miss Cooper's telling of it, you see. She's quite the *raconteuse*."

"Aha." Clearly Captain Vigo obviously didn't believe them, but since he was unwilling to contradict a passenger, he had no choice but to let it go.

"That was a close one," Addie said after he left. "We shall have to be more careful. I'm not supposed to show favoritism among the guests, for one thing."

"Oh, so last night was simply a regular passenger perk?" Clara teased, shocked at her own daring.

Addie blushed and smiled at her sheepishly. "Certainly not, and you know it. No one can stop me from *having* favorites, I simply need to hide it better."

A buzzy sort of happiness blossomed in Clara's chest as she looked at Addie. She couldn't believe how much different she felt from yesterday. If someone as beautiful and charming as Addie thought Clara was worth her time, perhaps she was more than just Clumsy Clara after all.

It was difficult to concentrate on what the guide was saying during their day of sightseeing. Instead, her mind was planted firmly back in her stateroom with Addie. There was still another week of the trip to go, and the possibility of future such encounters was tantalizing.

CHAPTER NINE

Having accomplished her mission of seducing Clara far more quickly than she'd thought, Addie was at loose ends as to how to occupy herself for the rest of the trip. She saw no point in deepening her connection with Clara. There was certainly no practical reason to do so. Clara was struggling to figure out how she would support herself, let alone a companion. Addie's current position paid reasonably well, provided her with a place to live, and gave her the opportunity to meet many wealthy travelers. It would be foolish to even consider giving that up.

She couldn't justify getting to know Clara better on an emotional level, either. It had been a ridiculous flight of fancy to open up to her as much as she had, both in Lyon and the night before on the observation deck. That was practically asking to be hurt. Soon, Clara would return to America and seldom think of Addie at all, except perhaps as a fun memory of her vacation.

As the passengers returned from a busy day of touring castles and little villages, Clara was notified that she had a telegram. When she returned to the deck, she made a beeline for Addie and practically skipped up to her.

"Hello, Add—Miss Barnes," she said cheerfully, her brown eyes shining brightly. "Isn't it a lovely evening?"

"Yes indeed, Miss Cooper," Addie said, nonplussed. It was as warm and muggy as the previous nights, but clearly, something had brought a smile to Clara's face.

"Clara, do stop prancing around like that," Matilda Cooper said sternly. "Anyone would think you were a…a showgirl or something. George Broderick will arrive at any moment."

"George Broderick can think whatever he likes. That's not my concern," Clara said evenly. There was a note of defiance in her tone that Addie had never heard before.

Mrs. Cooper looked at her niece as if she was a stranger. "What in the world has gotten into you, my girl?"

Clara ignored the question and turned back to Addie.

"Won't you dine with us tonight, Miss Barnes?" she asked.

"I'm afraid I can't, Miss Cooper," Addie said, feeling Matilda Cooper's beady eyes on her. "It wouldn't be proper for me to dine with the guests."

"Surely, you can make an exception?" Clara pressed hopefully. "I'm ordering champagne."

"I would be happy to join you for luncheon tomorrow when we're not aboard ship. Would that do?"

"I suppose that will have to suffice," Clara said. She sounded slightly disappointed, but there was still an extra spring in her step as she walked into the dining room. Addie couldn't fathom what had inspired it.

Addie's curiosity continued to mount, and at last, she could bear it no longer. While the guests were at dinner, she crept to Clara's cabin and let herself in with her passkey, locking the door behind her. At first glance, it looked the same as ever, but after a quick search, she found a telegram in Clara's jewelry case. That had to be it; there had been such a monumental shift in Clara's behavior, it must have been caused by some external news. She quickly read the telegram.

Will read this morning STOP Horrible Hank not so horrible STOP Left you all 500k of his estate STOP Happy days ahead STOP Love Albie and Fred.

Addie's eyebrows rose high as she slid the telegram back inside its hiding place. Obviously, Horrible Hank referred to Clara's grandfather. Addie smirked as she imagined the look on Matilda Cooper's face when she learned the news. No wonder Clara's whole demeanor had changed. She was no longer dependent on finding a husband or relying on wealthier relatives to support her. What Clara and Matilda had thought would be a small token legacy was, in fact, a life-changing amount.

Clara wasn't the only one whose plans were affected by the news. If she lived even slightly modestly, the amount would be more than enough to keep her *and* a companion in comfort for life. Being Clara Cooper's kept girl was a promising long-term prospect indeed.

Assuming, that was, that Addie could get Clara to offer. She carefully placed Clara's jewelry box back in the exact position where she'd found it, her mind whirring.

CHAPTER TEN

Clara's head was so in the clouds after receiving the telegram that she had to repeatedly look for signs that she was, in fact, awake and not in the throes of an overly elaborate daydream. The fifth time she pulled the message from the envelope, it gave her a paper cut, and the stinging served as a valuable reminder that this was real. For the first time on the trip, she was grateful for Aunt Matilda's presence. No fantasy she could possibly whip up in her overactive imagination would ever include her aunt.

It was no dream or hallucination, nor was it some mean-hearted prank. No one but her brothers would have known their shared nickname for their grandfather, and though they both loved a good joke as much as the next person, neither of them would be cruel enough to fool her about something so important.

No, she was free to accept the fact that she was now the recipient of a veritable fortune. She was confused as to why her grandfather had chosen to bestow it on her when he had never even laid eyes on her, but she could try to puzzle that out later. For now, she wanted to revel in this most surprising turn of events.

The day had not had an especially auspicious beginning. She had been hoping to sneak off with Addie during the excursion, but Addie had stayed behind on the boat due to her worries about the captain's scrutiny at breakfast. Aunt Matilda had been especially bossy and condescending on the bus ride back to the port, and Clara had scarcely resisted the urge to throttle her.

Hearing that she had a telegram had alarmed her at first. Transatlantic messages were expensive, and she couldn't imagine anyone she knew sending one unless the news was dire. Visions of something horrible having befallen her parents or one of her brothers had filled her head as she'd waited for the telegraph operator to hand her the message. It had seemed to take an age for him to find it and for her to open it.

She'd mouthed the words that would change her life as she'd read them, the meaning not sinking in at first. Once they had, she'd had to clap a hand over her mouth to keep from screaming in both shock and joy. Instead, she'd sunk to her knees right there in the little communications office.

The telegraph operator had leapt to his feet and let out a torrent of alarmed-sounding French. He'd spoken too fast for Clara to understand most of it except for *le docteur*.

"No need for *le docteur*, I'm fine," she'd said, a hysterical giggle escaping. She'd clutched the telegram to her chest and accepted the man's proffered hand to help her up.

Back in her cabin, she'd done a little dance, unable to sit still. Wild possibilities had flashed across her mind in quick succession. Last night, she had been fantasizing about this very situation, although she couldn't have foreseen the circumstances that led to it. Once she returned home and the dust settled, she would be curious to learn what had caused her grandfather to change his mind and his will in her favor.

For now, she wished that she could celebrate with her family, by which she meant her parents and brothers. Aunt Matilda barely counted and would doubtlessly be upset at Clara inheriting the Cooper fortune. Now she could spend the rest of the trip knowing she had resources of her own, that she no longer needed to make sure she stayed in her aunt's good graces. Ultimate freedom: whatever his reasoning, that was what her grandfather had given her.

With her family out of reach across the ocean and Aunt Matilda ruled out as a confidante, she was desperate to tell *someone* the startling news. She was halfway out the door of her cabin in search of Addie when something gave her pause. Was it wise to trust her with such important news when they barely knew each other? It might be better to spend more time with Addie before opening up to her.

She could still celebrate with Addie after a fashion, even if she didn't tell her the full story. She had planned to order champagne to share with her, but Addie's refusal to join her for dinner had quashed that idea. It was disappointing after already spending the entire day apart.

Not even that could dampen her spirits now, though. All evening, she felt like she was floating, miles away from the boring dinner and uninspired bridge game with the Brodericks. She was too happy and excited to worry about what George Broderick thought of her.

❖

Shortly after Clara retired to her cabin, there was a gentle tapping at the door, so light she thought at first it was just the wind. After a pause, it began again, and she opened the door a crack to see Addie out on the deck.

"May I come in?" Addie whispered. She was wearing silky black pajamas and fluffy white bedroom slippers, hardly suitable apparel for a casual nighttime stroll. She also had a bottle of peach nectar and two glasses.

Wordlessly, Clara stepped aside to let her in, carefully closing the door with a soft click and turning the lock.

"I'm sorry about declining dinner earlier," Addie said quietly, a penitent look on her face. "I was paranoid. Your aunt…well, no matter. Forgive me?"

"Of course," Clara said.

Addie carefully poured out two glasses of juice, then handed one to her. "I noticed how much you liked it at breakfast the other day."

Clara was touched by the thoughtfulness. She took a sip, letting the delicious nectar sit on her tongue before setting the glass on her nightstand.

Addie watched her hungrily as she swallowed, then leaned forward and kissed her. Clara kissed her back, pulling her down on the bed beside her. They traded kisses back and forth for a while. After Addie's tongue darted in and out of her mouth a few times, Clara hesitantly tried sliding her own into Addie's mouth. Addie moaned quietly, and Clara repeated the action with a little more confidence.

She fumbled at the buttons of Addie's pajama top until Addie was able to shrug out of it, the low light of the lamp sending a golden glow over her breasts. Clara stared at them for a few moments, captivated by the sight, then cupped them with trembling hands. Addie gasped as her nipples hardened under Clara's fingers.

Clara leaned down and took one in her mouth, running her tongue over it and sucking it gently while Addie bit back a moan. Clara hadn't had time to do anything for Addie during their earlier encounter, so she took her time now, savoring the hitch of Addie's breath and the way she buried her hands in Clara's hair.

"That feels so good," Addie panted.

The sound fueled Clara's desire even further, and she slid her hand inside Addie's pajama pants. "Oh," she said softly, parting Addie's cleft and stroking the slick heat she found there. As much as she'd enjoyed Addie touching her before, this was equally pleasurable in its own way. She explored Addie's body, drinking in the sight of her face as she touched her.

Addie cupped Clara's hand from outside her pants, gently guiding her movements. Clara felt a raised spot that caused Addie to hiss with pleasure and thrust her hips up, much as she herself had done earlier. She kept touching it like Addie had done to her, and before long, Addie was moaning her name in her ear, then slumping back on the bed.

"Did…did you like that?" she asked nervously. They hadn't spoken of it, but Addie seemed more experienced in such matters, and Clara hoped she'd been able to please her.

Addie giggled. "Of course I did. Couldn't you tell?" She kissed Clara deeply, then rolled on top of her. Her palms felt burning hot as she slowly pushed Clara's nightgown up, caressing her thighs.

Clara's breath stuttered in her throat as Addie settled between her legs. She felt Addie's warm breath on her core, then a rush of pleasure as her tongue touched her.

This time, it was her turn to thread her fingers through Addie's silky hair, tugging gently whenever the sensation got particularly overwhelming. She wished she could cry out from the flames coursing through her body caused by Addie's firm tongue, but she had enough of her wits about her to remember how vital it was that no one hear them. She stared at the ceiling, the sight of Addie's head nestled between her thighs too much to take in. Even still, it felt like far too soon before she was cresting over the edge to another release even more powerful than the one she'd felt earlier.

After she was done, she pulled Addie up beside her. There was an unfamiliar taste on her tongue when Clara kissed her, and she realized she must be tasting herself. She wondered what Addie tasted like, but her eyelids felt heavy, and her body totally relaxed. There was still another week left of the trip. She'd get her chance later, she thought hazily as she drifted off.

CHAPTER ELEVEN

Their excursion the next day took them to a lavender farm. After an introduction from the farmer about the history of lavender cultivation in Provence, they were turned loose to roam the fields and cut some of the herb for themselves if they wanted to. It couldn't have been a finer day for it. The sun was shining, but it wasn't overly hot. Clara was eager to explore the farm, not least because Addie had come along on this particular excursion.

The farmer offered baskets and pruning shears to those who wanted them. Clara couldn't imagine Aunt Matilda squatting amid the endless rows of lavender cutting the fragrant stalks for herself and was unsurprised that her aunt refused the tools and loudly proclaimed that she would stay in the tea room and shop at the farmhouse.

"Would you care to accompany me, Miss Cooper?" Addie asked formally, winking at her. "I've been here before, and I can show you where the best plants are."

"Yes, I'd appreciate that," Clara said, winking back.

Addie came to stand beside her and gestured to the fields on their left. "Shall we?"

"Let's."

"There's a secret picnic spot in the far field that the workers use to hide from the bosses. I bribed one to get us a few hours alone there," Addie whispered as they started walking.

A thrill ran through Clara as they moved sedately among the rows of lavender, wandering farther from the rest of the group as if by chance. It felt like a grand romance from one of the novels she loved, like Lucy Honeychurch being romanced by George Emerson in Italy. Thankfully,

Aunt Matilda saw no reason to observe her closely in Addie's company, taking a break from her self-appointed chaperone duties.

Addie had brought her own basket from the boat. It looked suspiciously heavy and was covered with a red checkered cloth instead of being empty in anticipation of being filled with lavender.

"What did you bring?" Clara asked Addie once they were far enough from the others that she was confident no one could hear them.

"A bit of lunch and one of your sketchbooks and your pencils in case you want to draw anything."

Clara squeezed her hand, not even caring if anyone else saw. That was just like Addie, thoughtful enough to know that she'd be inspired in such a beautiful setting and need to try to draw it.

After a ten-minute walk, they found the picnic spot easily enough; it was the only place where the narrow rows of lavender plants widened enough for two to sit side by side. They took a quick glance around, but they were so far away from the entrance to the farm that they would be mere specks on the horizon to any watching eyes.

Addie unfurled the cloth, then knelt next to her basket. She laid out a bottle of red wine, a baguette, a wheel of cheese, and some succulent-looking grapes. There were even two wineglasses carefully wrapped in cloth napkins.

"You carried all this the whole time? It must have been heavy. You should have given it to me," Clara chided.

"Nonsense, that wouldn't have been very chivalrous of me," Addie said briskly, handing her a glass of wine. "Cheers."

They clinked glasses, and Clara took a tentative sip. She didn't know much about wine, but she was pleasantly surprised at the way the taste flowed smoothly over her tongue.

"Do you like it?" Addie asked, watching her drink more deeply this time.

Clara nodded. "It's good. I've never really had wine before. Prohibition, you know. My parents aren't exactly the type to risk jail time for a bottle of merlot."

Addie grinned and started divvying up the food. "If I hadn't already been planning to head for Europe, that would've tipped me over the edge. It must be even worse where you live. Puritan influence and all that."

"I suppose so," Clara said, biting her lip as she thought before drinking more. "I haven't traveled outside of New England before, so I don't know how different it is. What's Chicago like? Aunt Matilda calls it a den of iniquity. But her standards…well, you've seen how she is."

"Oh, I'm sure it's not all that different, really. People are just people, wherever you go," Addie said. "Would you like some more?"

Clara held out her glass, surprised to see that she'd almost finished the wine already. Her head felt pleasantly buzzy. "Are you from the city itself or a suburb?"

"The city." Addie had already finished her second glass of wine, but Clara supposed she probably had a higher tolerance, being more accustomed to it.

"What neighborhood?" She realized how little she knew of Addie's life before she'd come abroad. She wanted to learn everything, every detail that had shaped Addie into the person she was. "Aunt Matilda used to travel there with Uncle Henry on his business trips. Perhaps she knows it."

"Oh, don't let's talk about ancient history," Addie said with a smile. "There are so many more interesting things to do than talk about my boring life. For instance, you've never made love in a lavender field in Provence, have you?"

"N…no," Clara stuttered, feeling heat rise to her cheeks.

Addie grinned roguishly. "Neither have I. We'd better remedy that."

Afterward, they lay in a stupor, the sun beating down on their skin as insects hummed and buzzed around. The scent of the lavender filled the air, strong but not overwhelming. Clara wished they could stay here forever, hidden from the world with no one to disappoint or to make demands of them. Addie's eyes were closed, and from her deep breathing, Clara could tell she was either asleep already or well on her way. She thought about joining her, but the scene was too beautiful not to try to capture.

She dragged herself upright and rummaged quietly in Addie's basket for her sketchbook and pencils. With gentle pencil strokes, she started outlining Addie's nude form. She couldn't feel the moment it happened, but she realized that whatever innate gift she had must have taken over. Her pencil ghosted over the page as if of its own accord, perfectly tracing the curve of Addie's cheek, the Cupid's bow of her lips. She drew faster and faster, recklessly shading in the flush on Addie's skin from the sun, the dark honey blond curls between her legs. Before she knew it, Addie was stirring and blinking her eyes against the sun.

"What are you drawing?" Addie mumbled sleepily.

"What's that?" Clara asked, not really listening as she put the finishing touches on the sprigs of lavender in the background of the portrait.

"Can I see?" Addie sat up, her breasts bumping gently against her ribcage as she moved. She held out her hand.

Clara looked at her finished work. So often she hated the things she made as soon as she was done, but there was something special about this one. She didn't immediately want to tear it up and toss it into the river, at any rate. Still, she felt awash with nerves as she handed it to Addie.

Addie stared at it for so long that Clara started to feel impatient rather than anxious. She resisted the urge to snatch it back protectively.

"Is this how you see me?" Addie asked softly, still looking at the drawing.

Clara shifted uncomfortably, wondering if she had revealed too much of herself and her own feelings. "It's just what you look like," she said, deflecting.

When Addie looked up at last, Clara was surprised to see that her eyes looked shiny, as if filled with unshed tears. She cleared her throat loudly, and Clara thought she must have imagined it. "I've never seen a drawing of myself before. It's a pity I can't show it to anyone."

"I suppose it would raise some eyebrows," Clara said. When Addie moved to hand it back to her, she shook her head. "No, you keep it."

"Are you sure? Well, thank you. I really do love it." Addie looked uncommonly shy, and they grinned at each other stupidly. Finally, Addie broke the silence by fumbling for her watch. "What time is it? Oh no, it's nearly three o'clock. We'd better be getting back."

They leapt into action, Addie struggling into her clothes and trying to fix her rumpled hair as Clara frantically tossed her pencils into the basket without bothering to put them back in their case.

"I think we've got everything," she said, biting her lip and looking around at the ground nervously for any forgotten items.

"Come here a moment." Addie reached up and pulled several strands of grass from Clara's hair before straightening her hat, then tilted her head up and kissed her tenderly. "That's better."

They were halfway back to the farmhouse when Clara clapped a hand to her forehead. "We didn't pick any lavender."

Addie gasped. "Oh, good thinking. Erm…here." She knelt next to a particularly full plant, grabbed the shears from the depths of her basket, and cut off nearly every sprig. There wasn't time to waste going along to different plants to choose more carefully.

"Poor thing," she said, patting the plant's now-naked stems. "I'm sorry. Your sacrifice was for a worthy cause."

"Yes, protecting us from the scrutiny of Aunt Matilda," Clara said, and they both giggled.

"In all seriousness," Addie said, panting slightly from the exertion of their brisk pace. "I think it'll probably be fine. Lavender is a strong plant, and I only cut it back a little more than a regular pruning."

"A new modern haircut," Clara said, and Addie laughed. The sound warmed her as thoroughly as the sun on her bare skin not long ago. "You know an awful lot about plants for someone who grew up in the city and lives on a boat now."

Addie shrugged. "I've read almost every book in the passengers' lounge. I like learning about all sorts of things. And one can't spend this much time in Provence and not know more than you ever wanted to about lavender."

They reached the farmhouse at last, where Aunt Matilda was looking around nervously.

"There you are. Clara, I declare, you will be the death of me. I thank God every day that I never had any daughters of my own."

Clara was also grateful for her nonexistent female cousins' sakes. Having Aunt Matilda as a mother was a prospect too horrible to contemplate. They piled into the waiting car, Aunt Matilda forcing herself in between Clara and Addie as she kept up a running monologue about Girls These Days.

❖

With Matilda sitting between them, Addie and Clara weren't able to talk freely anymore. Addie was grateful for it. Her head ached from the wine and the long time she'd spent lying in the sun, and she was eager for nothing more than a cool shower back on the boat. More than that, though, she needed some time away from Clara.

The drawing had shaken her deeply, more than she cared to admit. As soon as she was back in her cabin, she pulled the little curtain around her bunk closed and took it out of her basket. Occasionally, she felt flickers of guilt at how she was using Clara, but right now, it was an all-out conflagration. Clara's skill seemed to have grown by leaps and bounds during the trip, and it was on full display in her depiction of Addie.

The lavender plants looked lifelike, the rich purple popping off the page. She could practically feel the gentle breeze causing them to sway. The sun's golden rays seemed to dance off her sketched form as she lay asleep on the checkered cloth. She looked…the only word her mind would produce was *angelic*. If her face really did relax into a gentle smile in sleep, she had no way of knowing. More likely, Clara had been influenced by her affection for her.

She wished she really was the person Clara saw, but she couldn't stand the idea of being that vulnerable ever again. She had trusted her family to love her unconditionally, and they had let her down. She had given Eva her heart, fully and truly, but Eva's death had revealed how fragile the happiness they had shared really was. Even if she wanted to return Clara's feelings without reservation, she wasn't sure she still knew how.

What did Clara expect from her, anyway? Even as sheltered as she was, she couldn't possibly think that Addie had really fallen head over heels for a random tourist she had met on the job. Surely, she had some idea of the true nature of their relationship. Besides, if Addie was really the first romance she'd ever had, she would eventually learn that the novelty wore off. Before she knew it, she'd be tired of Addie and looking for someone new.

It was important for Addie to protect herself and her interests. All her experience had taught her that no one else would, so it was down to her to take care of herself. They said all was fair in love and war, so she needed to harden her heart and do whatever she could to secure her future.

CHAPTER TWELVE

Although the busy schedule and close quarters made it difficult, Clara and Addie snuck away every chance they got. Addie was ingenious at coming up with hiding places and excuses for why they both needed to leave the rest of the group. Clara wondered if she had done this before with other passengers. She thought of all the time Addie had spent with Miss Windermere and felt a flash of jealousy. Of course, Miss Windermere had had her own palatial stateroom and no nosy chaperone breathing down her neck, so Addie wouldn't have needed to be so secretive.

Luckily, Addie had made arrangements with the chief engineer of the ship. Unlike her, he had his own private bunkroom and didn't mind if she used it when he was working. In exchange, she kept him supplied with various gourmet foods and bottles of wine smuggled out of the passengers' dining room where no one who worked belowdecks was allowed.

Over the course of the trip, Clara grew as familiar with the engineer's bunkroom as she did with Addie's body. She shed her shyness about physical intimacy, but she was slower to reveal her innermost thoughts. She was still acutely conscious of how much more worldly and experienced Addie was, and she dreaded making a fool of herself. Maybe it shouldn't have mattered, since they'd probably never see each other again after the trip ended. She wasn't so delusional as to think they had any kind of a future together, even with her newfound wealth. Still, she wanted Addie to remember her for the right reasons, and not because she was some yokel constantly revealing her naivety.

Often, she let Addie do most of the talking. She would regale

Clara with stories of her travels. Although she rarely mentioned her by name, Clara quickly realized that Addie had had most of her adventures with Eva. It took her an embarrassingly long time to connect the dots, but finally, she brought herself to ask Addie the question that lingered in her mind.

"You and Eva…you loved her, didn't you?"

Addie smiled sadly. "Yes. We were together for four years. We were very happy together, but she contracted diphtheria and died a few days later. It happened so quickly."

"How awful," Clara said, squeezing her hand.

"It was." Addie sniffed loudly and dabbed at her eyes with a knuckle. "But anyway, that's enough about me. What about your past romantic escapades?"

"I went to a few dances with a friend of my brother's, but that was about it," Clara confessed. "He asked if he could call on me, but I said no. He was very nice, but we didn't have much in common aside from Fred, and that didn't seem like enough somehow. Then he got a job that sent him to San Francisco, and that was that."

"The young men of Willoughby didn't exactly make a lasting impression on you, then," Addie said. Her tone was teasing, but there was a friendly twinkle in her eyes that told Clara she wasn't mocking her.

"No. Are you…have you…" Clara trailed off, too embarrassed to finish the question. She fiddled with the clasp of Aunt Matilda's emerald necklace, which she'd stealthily borrowed to impress Addie. Thankfully, Addie seemed to read her mind.

"I only like women," she said matter-of-factly.

Clara nodded as if it was a perfectly ordinary sentiment, but inwardly, she was reeling at the idea that it was even an option. She thought back to some of the particularly close friendships she'd had at school, the way she'd sometimes felt shy and nervous around those girls in a way she never did with all the young men her family shoved at her. "I think maybe I do too," she said quietly.

Addie rolled onto her side to face her and propped herself up on her elbow. "That must be rather inconvenient for you. I can earn my living, at least. I suppose you'll end up married to some man out of necessity. Hopefully, not one too odious."

Clara bit her lip, unsure how to respond. Much as she liked Addie, she was hesitant to reveal her inheritance. She liked their—

acquaintance? friendship?—as it was, without the addition of money into the mix. As long as Addie didn't know about the money, Clara could be sure she genuinely liked her. "I'm hoping that won't be necessary," she said at last.

"Well, if you decide you'd rather work for a living, I'd be happy to advise you," Addie said with a wry laugh.

Clara wasn't sure if she was serious or not, but it gave her an idea. "What would you think…"

Addie raised her eyebrows expectantly.

"Would it be all right if I wrote to you after I go home?"

A flash of what looked like disappointment crossed Addie's face, but then, she was smiling, and Clara thought she must have imagined it. "Yes, of course. In fact, I'll be quite disappointed if you don't. I…I'm going to miss you very much."

Clara beamed, happiness ballooning in her chest despite the dread of their parting the next day. "I'll miss you too. I wish the trip was longer."

"So do I," Addie said sadly. "I suppose we'll just have to make the most of the time we have left." She stretched her arms over her head and arched her back like a cat, which pushed her breasts out in a way that drove all thoughts of their previous conversation from Clara's mind.

❖

Aunt Matilda was waiting when Clara returned to her cabin. "Where on earth have you been? Have you seen my emerald necklace?" she demanded. "I wore it to dinner tonight, and now I simply cannot find it anywhere."

Clara clapped a hand to her neck to try to hide the necklace from Aunt Matilda's view, knowing how upset her aunt would be at her taking it without permission. To her dismay, it wasn't there. She surreptitiously patted around in case it had gotten tucked under the neckline of her dress, but it was gone. "I don't know where it is," she said truthfully. Most likely, it had fallen off in the engineer's bunkroom. With any luck, she could go retrieve it and then "find" it in an obscure spot in Aunt Matilda's cabin. "I'll go look for it."

"Don't bother," Aunt Matilda said. "I've already alerted the captain that it was probably stolen. He is undertaking a search of the ship right now, starting in the crew bunks."

"Why start there?" Clara said nervously. "Isn't it more likely that it just…fell off somewhere, the dining room or the lounge, maybe?"

"*Tuh.* Probably one of these crew members thought he could get away with stealing it on the last night, thinking I wouldn't notice. Well, he won't."

"I'll go see how the search is going," Clara said, panic rising. If she could only get to the engineer's bunk before Captain Vigo did…

"You'll stay right where you are," Aunt Matilda said sternly. "Vanishing at all hours, talking back, I really don't know *what* your mother will say when we get home." She stood in front of the door with her arms folded, looking at Clara disapprovingly. There was no way to leave without pushing past her, which wouldn't help the situation. There was nothing to do but wait and pray that the necklace had fallen out of sight.

To her abject horror, Captain Vigo himself knocked on the door a few minutes later, Aunt Matilda's necklace in his hand and a somber expression on his face.

"Oh thank you, thank you," she said, fluttering around as he handed it to her. "Wherever did you find it?"

"In a crew member's bunk, madame. Don't worry, he will be dismissed immediately," he said. "Would you like to alert the police?"

Clara winced and knew she had to speak up. She couldn't let the poor man lose his livelihood because of her mistake, possibly even go to prison. "Actually…" she said, and both her aunt and Vigo turned to look at her. "Aunt Matilda, *I* took the necklace. I know I shouldn't have, but it was so pretty, and I wanted to wear it just for a little bit. I didn't think you'd notice. Then I was exploring the ship, and it must have fallen off."

"And why," Aunt Matilda said, staring beadily at her as she over enunciated each word. "Why, exactly, would you have been wearing my necklace in a crew member's bunk? Clara, have you been…*cavorting* with a seaman?"

"No, of course not," Clara said. Aunt Matilda clearly didn't believe her, and Clara couldn't blame her. Without the added context of Addie, it looked terrible. She knew the true nature of their relationship would never occur to Aunt Matilda, but she wasn't so sure about the captain. She had to come up with some sort of explanation without dragging Addie into it.

While she was scrambling her brain trying to think of a remotely believable lie, she heard footsteps rushing down the deck. They stopped right in front of her door, and moments later, Addie was barreling into the cabin.

"I took the necklace," she said, panting from exertion. She must have run all the way up here from the crew bunks. "Miss Cooper was in my bunk for a visit, and when she left, I saw it had come loose. I thought...I was going to return it, but it was so beautiful, and Mrs. Cooper has so many lovely things. I didn't think she'd even notice it was missing, just for the evening. But when I heard that they were coming to search for it, I got scared that it would be discovered, so I hid it in another bunk. I just knew Cla—Miss Cooper would confess, and I knew how it would look. I can't let her take the blame for something I did."

Clara tried and probably failed to make her expression look like Addie's story wasn't a total lie. Aunt Matilda and the captain were seemingly too busy staring at Addie in shock to notice Clara's face.

"Mademoiselle Barnes, I never would have thought it of you," Captain Vigo said severely, and Addie hung her head. "Of course you'll be dismissed without a reference."

As kind as it was for Addie to fall on her sword, Clara couldn't allow it. She opened her mouth to protest, but Addie glanced at her and shook her head minutely.

Aunt Matilda glared at Addie. "Truly, Miss Barnes, I would have expected better of someone of your disposition. It seems I was wrong about you. I will not be pressing criminal charges because I am a good Christian woman, and I believe in forgiveness, but I shall warn all of my acquaintances about you."

"She isn't even the one who took it," Clara burst out. "And you heard her, she was going to return it."

"So *she* says," Aunt Matilda said nastily. "As if you can believe a word of it. And what was she doing in that man's bunk, I'd like to know. *Tuh.*"

Clara's fear was gone, overshadowed by growing anger at Aunt

Matilda's smug sanctimony. She knew from long experience that arguing back was useless, but there must be something she could do to help Addie.

After the captain had sent Addie belowdecks with strict orders not to leave her bunk room until they docked in Port-Saint-Louis the next day, he apologized again to Aunt Matilda and bid them both a good night.

Clara packed Aunt Matilda's belongings, seething silently as her aunt tutted and *tuhed* about the perils of trusting the lower classes. She longed to whip out the telegram and wave it in Aunt Matilda's face, but she didn't want to risk it until she was in Paris and could get to an international bank to access the money. As quickly as she could, she finished her task and went back to her own cabin, promising Aunt Matilda that she was going straight to bed. She waited until she was sure her aunt had fallen asleep, then crept out and took the now-familiar route down to the crew cabins.

"Oh! I didn't know if I'd get a chance to see you again," Addie said, looking up in surprise as Clara entered her room. Her suitcase was on her narrow bed, mostly filled already.

Clara felt a pang in her chest at the sight. This had been Addie's home, and it had taken her less than half an hour to pack up everything she owned. She was losing her position through no fault of her own, only to protect Clara. Wordlessly, Clara strode forward and swept Addie into her arms, kissing her desperately.

"What was that for?" Addie asked softly once they had finally broken apart, brushing a stray hair out of Clara's eyes.

"You shouldn't have done that," Clara said. "I would have been all right. My aunt might have thought a little worse of me, but now you've lost your position, your home…"

"I'll be fine," Addie said, although Clara could detect worry in her eyes. "It'll work out for me somehow, it always does. I just couldn't let you be blamed. I knew, with it being in a man's room, your reputation…I can find another position, but you would be in a terrible jam if word got out. No respectable man would want to marry you, and then you'd, what, be under Matilda's thumb forever? That's no life for you."

"That's why you did it?" Clara asked, anguished. Addie had thrown it all away for nothing. "Oh, dear, no. You really needn't have done it. I didn't want to tell you until…well, I was waiting to tell you, but I got a telegram last week. My grandfather's estate has finally been settled, and I'm getting an inheritance, more than enough to live on. I don't need to get married at all unless I choose to. You protected me for nothing."

She could hardly bear to watch Addie's face as she delivered the news. Addie pulled herself free and sank slowly onto her bunk, looking shell-shocked. Clara pushed the suitcase aside so she could sit next to her.

"Addie, darling? I'm so sorry. I should have said something sooner, told you, or said more to the captain. I can go talk to him now, maybe there's still a chance for you to keep your post."

"Don't bother," Addie said hollowly. "I made my choice, and I shall abide by it, unnecessary sacrifice or not. Only…would you perhaps be a reference for me? Your aunt knows a great many people, and I'm afraid her warning will go far. I know it might be a bit untruthful to say I worked for you, but I'd be grateful for even just a character reference. Perhaps then, I can go into service or even be a paid companion again if I'm lucky." She cleared her throat and sat up straight, something of her usual poise and dignity settling around her shoulders.

The sight broke Clara's heart even more than Addie's previous downtrodden demeanor. She would give anything in the world to bring a smile back to Addie's face, and inspiration struck.

"I can do better than that," she said excitedly. "You could come back to America with me when I leave tomorrow. The legacy from my grandfather is enough for me to afford a nice little home somewhere and hire a companion. Then you can live with me in a respectable position."

Addie beamed, but her face turned uncertain. "Oh, I'd love that. But don't feel obligated to hire me out of guilt. I would hate to make things difficult for you with your family. And surely, after a while, you might change your mind about getting married, or want a, ah, change in companions."

"Aunt Matilda won't like it, but I don't need to care about what she thinks anymore. Everyone in the family knows what she's like. If I vouch for you, they'll give you a chance." She grasped Addie's hands, threading their fingers together. "Say you'll come with me. Please? It's not out of guilt. I *want* you with me." She held her breath, her heart racing from showing such emotional vulnerability.

Addie stared at their clasped hands, then nodded. "All right, but under one condition."

"Anything," Clara promised.

"If you start to tire of me, please tell me and send me on my way. I know you feel responsible for me, and you're far too kind to do so ordinarily, but I don't want to stay where I'm not wanted."

"I'll agree. But I could never tire of you."

Sunlight broke through the clouds on Addie's face, and they were both giggling.

"Is this really happening?" Addie asked joyfully. "Pinch me, I must be dreaming." Clara obliged her, and their laughter intensified before dropping off as they clutched at each other.

Their tryst was cut short when Marian, one of Addie's bunkmates, returned. They broke away from each other hurriedly, but Marian merely rolled her eyes and collapsed onto her own bed, seemingly too exhausted to comment.

Clara couldn't stop smiling as she fixed the buttons on her blouse. Addie was coming back with her, had promised an entire year to her. Somehow, what had seemed one of the bleakest evenings of her life had blossomed into the most magical.

❖

She had done it. Exhilaration and relief coursed through Addie all night, keeping her from sleeping. She had thrown all her chips into the pot and bluffed her way to victory. She had been on her way to Clara's cabin to return the necklace when the idea had revealed itself to her, and it went as smoothly as she could have wished. Busby Berkeley couldn't have choreographed it better, from Clara's partial confession to Matilda's angry bluster.

The hardest part by far had been waiting in her cabin, feeling in her heart that Clara would come but not quite sure until she saw her in the doorway. Even then, she wasn't sure it was going to work; she had still had to prod Clara in the direction of offering her a paid companionship. At last, she had, and Addie had played her part perfectly, the proud poor girl not wanting to impose on her wealthier lover.

If her plan had failed, she would have been in dire straits: no job, no reference, nowhere to live, barely any savings, and in a foreign land to boot. Now she needed to make sure she stayed in Clara's good graces for as long as possible. She was under no delusions that Clara would want her around forever, but at least she had bought herself a reprieve from struggling.

A few years ought to be enough time to get what she could out of Clara and find a soft landing place once Clara got sick of her. As a lover, Clara was generous and eager to please. Addie found her company enjoyable too. Sure, she was a bit naive and far too trusting, but those traits could be refreshing sometimes and would make it easier for Addie to depart on good terms.

If anything, she worried she was a little too comfortable around Clara. It wouldn't do to let her guard down for even a moment. Her experiences with Eva and Hester had amply demonstrated that her luck could change on a dime. The only person she could rely on was herself.

To the surprise of no one, Matilda Cooper was dismayed and alarmed by the news that Addie would be returning with them. Her muttered imprecations, liberally sprinkled with *tuhs*, continued all the way to the Lyon train station. At last, she seemed to have tired herself out, or perhaps finally accepted defeat in the face of her niece's continued defiance. She begrudgingly allowed Addie to sit in their compartment with them, although she ostentatiously checked on her jewelry several times an hour.

Clara was only able to afford a third-class train ticket for Addie, since she wouldn't have access to her inheritance until they reached Paris, and Matilda steadfastly refused to contribute a cent. She was profusely apologetic, but Addie reassured her over and over that she didn't mind, that it was a privilege to be there at all.

At the last stop before they reached Paris, the train stopped long enough for them to leave the station for lunch. Addie had enough francs stored away to treat Clara to a meal at a little café. On their way back to the station, a young man started following them, leering and calling out suggestively. Clara tensed, nearly frozen with fear. Addie unleashed every swear word Eva had ever taught her in French, Italian, and German, and he soon broke away, looking both amused and slightly alarmed.

"Oh my," Clara said, dabbing at her brow with her handkerchief. "That was quite alarming. I only recognized a few words of what you said. Son of a…what did that other word mean?"

"I called him a son of a whore," Addie said primly, trying not to laugh at the look of horror and embarrassment on Clara's face. "And I won't tell you what the rest of it means."

"Please don't," Clara said vehemently.

Addie shrugged as they started walking again. "You never know when it might come in handy, like just now."

"I sincerely hope it never does again," Clara said, shaking her head. "I had always liked the idea of living in France, but not if something like that is a regular occurrence. Speaking of which, have you any idea of where you'd like to live?"

Addie looked at her in surprise. "Don't you want to live in Willoughby near your family?"

"I don't know. This trip has made me realize how much bigger the world is, you know? Oh, that sounds foolish, of course the world is big. But I would like to see more places, explore more. I love my parents and my brothers very much, of course, but they don't really understand. And to be honest, while they enjoy my company, they don't…*need* me around. If we wanted to live in, say, Boston, they would get along just fine without me."

"I would like living in Boston very much," Addie said, keeping her voice as even as she could. High society, fine boutiques, even clubs for other like-minded people? It would suit her needs perfectly. "Or if you're interested in a really big adventure, we could even go to New York."

Clara's eyes widened. "New York? I don't know, that's awfully far away. Maybe *too* far. I'd have to think about it. I suppose we needn't decide right now anyway."

"It has the advantage of two hundred miles between us and Matilda," Addie pointed out as they entered the train station.

"That's a terrible thing to say, but you make a good point," Clara said, snickering before forcing her face into an expression of solemn piety as the subject herself came into view.

Although she never went so far as to say it openly, Matilda was clearly furious that her late father-in-law's will had removed any standing she had to dictate Clara's choices. Addie wondered what had changed the old man's mind. Perhaps the loss of his favored older son had made him realize he'd been overly harsh on Clara's father, and this was his way of making amends. Whatever the reason, Matilda had been struck dumb by the news, and that alone was reason to thank the late Mr. Cooper.

They spent a few days in Paris before their ship was to depart for Boston from Calais. Clara went to the bank and withdrew enough money to purchase a second-class ticket on the same ship. She planned to join Addie there rather than booking a first-class cabin alongside Matilda. It wouldn't be as luxurious in second class, but Addie was more than willing for the trade-off of not seeing Matilda much during the journey.

Addie took Clara to see as many of the sights as they could fit in: the Eiffel Tower, the Louvre, a half-priced matinee show in the theater district. Clara stared at everything wide-eyed, looking awed at Addie's knowledge of the city. She especially loved the Eiffel Tower, spending ages looking out at the sprawling city. They stayed at the top long enough to watch the sunset and see the city light up below.

Some places, though, were too sacred to share. Addie kept to herself the Marais street where she had lived with Eva, the little café that made the best croissants in France and where they had breakfasted every Sunday. They didn't go to the underground dance club where she and Eva had spent most Friday nights, where they were able to hold each other close and dance.

She hadn't been back to the city since Eva's mother had thrown her out of the flat, and grief smacked her in the face at every turn. It was all she could do not to bark at Clara that she could not possibly care about whether they went to the Tuileries Garden before or after Notre-Dame when Eva, the most vibrant person she'd ever known, lay dead three hundred miles away.

She supposed she could have made some excuse to slip away long enough to visit Eva's grave at her family's villa near Basel, but she felt far closer to Eva here where they'd lived. The one time she had made the trip, hoping to feel a measure of peace, the pristine neatness of the cemetery had evoked a sense of emptiness that had nearly overwhelmed her. The dashed hope was like losing Eva all over again in a small way.

When Eva had moments of lucidity in her final days, she'd begged Addie to have her buried here in Paris. "It's the only place that's ever felt like home," she'd said. Her family had had different ideas, insisting on bringing her remains back to the place she had been so eager to leave.

"Are you all right?"

"What?" Addie snapped, her attention yanked back to the café where she was sitting.

Clara recoiled, an expression of hurt surprise on her face. "I asked if you were all right. You seemed…very far away."

"I'm sorry, Clarabella," Addie said, forcing a conciliatory smile onto her face. "I got lost in my own mind, I'm afraid. What were we talking about before my silly brain wandered away?"

Clara's face cleared, and she smiled shyly into her teacup, a blush rising to her cheeks as it did every time Addie used the pet name.

The sight sent a prickle of guilt down Addie's spine. Was she perhaps taking this too far? After all, Clara was hardly a canny woman of the world, able to distinguish the truth about their relationship. Perhaps Addie should pull back a bit before Clara got too emotionally attached.

"We were discussing what time we should leave for the station, and whether you get seasick on big ocean liners," Clara said.

Addie did not, it turned out, get seasick on ocean liners. Clara herself felt green around the gills for the first day, and mostly stayed in bed while Addie read to her and brought her cups of tea.

"This one has mint in it," Addie said, handing her another mug. "It helps settle the stomach."

"Thank you. Urgh," Clara said, covering her eyes as the room lurched again. "It's odd, you would think a bigger ship would be better, and yet the riverboat didn't cause me any trouble at all."

"Well, the ocean is a lot more turbulent, even on a big ship like this," Addie pointed out. "Did you get seasick on the way over too?"

Clara took a sip of the mint tea. She didn't know if it was psychological, but she thought she felt a little better. "I did for a few hours, but I don't recall it being this bad."

"Maybe you blocked out the memory of it, the way they say women do about childbirth. Otherwise, you would have had to stay in Europe for the rest of your life," Addie said with a laugh.

"Not that that would be so much of a hardship, but it'll be nice to be home. How long has it been since you were back?"

"Oh, nearly seven years now," Addie said, examining her fingernails.

"We could go to Chicago if you want," Clara suggested. "To see your family?"

Addie pressed her lips into a thin line. "That won't be necessary."

"Are you sure? I wouldn't mind. It would be lovely to meet your par—"

"I said no," Addie said sharply. "I don't want to go back there."

Clara forgot her seasickness in her rush to make amends. "I'm sorry. I didn't mean to upset you. I thought perhaps you didn't want to impose by asking, but clearly, I was wrong."

Addie sat on the edge of the bed and gripped Clara's hands. "Oh dear, I'm the one who's sorry. I've been simply beastly to you, and you didn't do anything wrong. The truth is…"

She stared at their clasped hands and took a deep breath. "My parents, my entire family…they're dead. The Spanish flu in 1918 took them one by one. First my father, then my older sister, my mother, both of my brothers. Finally, it was just my younger sister and me. I tried so hard to protect her, but I failed."

Her voice broke, and she gently tugged her hands free from Clara's to cover her face, her shoulders shaking. Clara sat up and pulled Addie into her arms. She'd noticed that Addie seemed reluctant to talk about her family, but never had she imagined such tragedy in her past.

She thought of Addie being all alone in the world and fought back a shiver. Yes, Addie was beautiful and charming and witty, all the things Clara wasn't, but Clara wouldn't have traded places with her for anything. She stroked Addie's hair and kissed the top of her head tenderly.

They didn't discuss Addie's family again for the rest of the voyage, keeping themselves occupied in other ways. The ship had copies of the

Boston Globe from as recently as two weeks ago, and they devoted hours to poring over real estate listings. Clara was eager to try living in the big city. After her adventures in Europe, she couldn't imagine going back to living in sleepy little Willoughby. Addie, with her experience of Paris and Chicago, liked the idea. She also pointed out that people were less likely to scrutinize their relationship in Boston than in Willoughby.

The idea made Clara feel a little funny. After all, someone as wonderful as Addie had chosen *her*, and she wanted to shout it from the rooftops. But she knew Addie was right, and they had to keep up appearances of being merely friends. She wished she could tell her immediate family. Her father, with his artistic temperament, might be understanding, and she thought her brothers might even be happy for her if they had time to get used to the idea. Her mother, though, would be horrified that her baby girl was abandoning the possibility of a husband and children.

If only she could discuss telling her family with Addie, weigh the pros and cons together. It struck her as insensitive to bring it up with someone whose own family had been lost so tragically, though. She would have to keep her own counsel.

It felt surreal to be circling listings in the newspaper for apartments that cost more to rent than her father made in a month. She reminded herself over and over again that she could afford it now, that it really wasn't all that extravagant. Her head spun when she thought about all the things she could buy that she had never even dared to daydream about before. Dresses, shoes, jewelry, maybe even an automobile. Not that she knew how to drive. Her parents couldn't afford an automobile, but her brothers had learned to drive in the Army and could surely teach her.

She chuckled at the thought of driving into Willoughby in a fancy car to go to the grocer or the hardware store. It was a simple town full of plain, hardworking people who didn't go in for flashiness or throwing money around. It was definitely for the best that she and Addie weren't planning on living there. Now that she had money, she wanted to spend some of it.

CHAPTER THIRTEEN

"Albie!" Clara flung herself into her oldest brother's embrace, laughing as their other brother, Fred, enveloped both of them in his long arms.

"Welcome home, sister dear," Albie said. "I hope you managed to retain your sanity after six weeks in our beloved Aunt Matilda's company."

"She must be spitting mad about the will," Fred added. "Harry was about ready to declare war on the lawyer's office, but the probate judge managed to convince him that the will was genuine."

"She's not pleased," Clara said, trying not to sound too smug. She stepped aside so Fred and Albie could see Addie. "Speaking of which…"

"Ah, the famous Miss Barnes," Albie said. "Or infamous, I should say. Matilda sent Mother a telegram ahead of time."

"Whatever she said, it's not true," Clara said indignantly. It wasn't really a surprise that Matilda had done so, but she resented it nevertheless. She wanted her family to get to know Addie without any prejudice instilled by Matilda.

"We know, we know," Albie said with a grin. He and Fred shook hands with Addie as they introduced themselves.

Their arrival was more excitement than the little Willoughby train station normally got, its passengers usually limited to businessmen commuting into the city during the week. The station was too small to have a porter to help them with their luggage, so Albie and Fred loaded it into a waiting taxi themselves.

It was surreal driving through the town where she'd spent her entire life. Her parents had never even owned an automobile, and now she could buy them a Duesenberg Model J if they wanted one. Every day of her first twenty-five years had been nearly the same, and now in the span of six weeks, everything had changed.

In less than ten minutes, they reached her parents' home. After all the grand castles, fine hotels, and well-appointed ships she'd experienced in Europe, the house she'd grown up in seemed even smaller and drabber. Wherever she and Addie moved, it would be far nicer.

She realized she was embarrassed for Addie to see the house and was instantly horrified with herself. It should take more than a surprise fortune and several weeks of Aunt Matilda's company to turn her into a snob, and she needed to be on her guard against such thoughts.

Once her parents came out to welcome them, she felt only joy in being reunited. They took turns hugging her, exclaiming over and over again how glad they were that she was home. Addie watched, a wistful expression on her face. Clara wondered if she was thinking of similar memories with her own parents.

They all gathered in the sitting room, and Clara basked in the warmth that always came from being with her family. They listened raptly as she and Addie described their adventures. At Addie's urging, she pulled out her sketchbook. Her parents and brothers gathered around to pore over it, exclaiming in delight at her drawings.

She wished she could have shown them her drawing of Addie from the lavender field; she still thought it was her best work yet. Her father was unlikely to be scandalized, having drawn plenty of nude models in life drawing classes over the years, but it would draw unwanted scrutiny to the exact nature of their relationship.

After they finished admiring her artwork, the subject changed to her new fortune.

"Have you any idea what changed Grandfather's mind about the will?" she asked.

Her brothers laughed but tried to look serious when their mother shot them a quelling look. "It seems that our dear cousin Harry had been, shall we say, *courting* the daughter of the judge he was clerking for," Albie said, still smirking.

"What would Grandfather find objectionable about that?" Clara asked, confused. If anything, it sounded like a suitable match that should have pleased him.

"Let's just say, there's going to be a wedding very soon, and a new addition to the happy couple much quicker than you'd expect," Fred said.

"Oh," Clara said, feeling herself blush as she grasped the implication.

"It's nothing to laugh at," her mother said sharply as her brothers snickered again. "Harry wouldn't have done the right thing if the girl's father hadn't forced him to. He's still denying responsibility and treating that poor young woman abominably. Imagine what kind of husband he'll be."

"Not to mention having Matilda as a mother-in-law," Addie muttered in Clara's ear.

That was a sobering thought indeed. Clara felt deep pity for her cousin's wife-to-be.

"Anyway, my father, being the pureblooded Puritan that he was, thoroughly disapproved," her father added. "Not that it should matter, of course, but he did feel strongly about such things. He was rather disgusted, both with the situation and with Harry's response to it. It seems he decided to wash his hands of all the Cooper men."

"Leaving you to pick up the pieces," Fred said cheerfully.

Although they'd be reluctant to accept money from her, Clara planned to insist on helping her parents and brothers financially. It wasn't as if she inherently deserved the inheritance any more than they did; it was Cooper family money, after all, and it might as well benefit all of them. She could sense no resentment from her brothers that they had been passed over in their grandfather's will, but it didn't feel right to keep it all to herself.

She and Addie would staying with her parents until they found an apartment. Since her parents' house didn't have an extra bedroom, Clara's father had set up a cot in her bedroom for Addie. They cuddled on Clara's twin bed before sleep.

"It's rather frightening when you think about it," Clara mused.

"Which part?" Addie asked, tracing indeterminate shapes onto her skin.

"Harry's fiancée. One day you're spending time with a man to see if you like him, the next, you're being dragged down the aisle and trapped in a miserable life."

Addie kissed her shoulder, her lips warm and tender. "Thank goodness we're safe from that fear. Maybe that's why your grandfather left you the money, so you'd never feel forced into a situation like that."

"Perhaps," Clara said, but she wasn't convinced his motivations were so altruistic. She thought it was far more likely to be about punishing the descendants who had disappointed him than doing something nice for her.

They had a busy day planned for tomorrow, so Addie soon returned to her own bed. They were going into Boston to do some shopping and visit Clara's favorite of the apartments they had read about.

Clara tried to sleep, but her mind was buzzing too much. She was full of anticipation for the next day. It signaled the start of her new life, a home of her own with Addie by her side. A small part of her was nervous, though. As unexciting as her life had been, at least it was predictable. No one wanted anything from her because she had nothing to give. Everything would be different now. At least she knew Addie loved her for who she was, not for her money. With that comforting thought, she finally dropped off to sleep.

CHAPTER FOURTEEN

"Ta-da," the stylist said, spinning the chair around to reveal a newly made over Clara.

"Do you like it?" Clara asked nervously, patting at her hair. Her eyes had been closed in, but she opened them now that she was facing away from the mirror.

Addie beamed. "You look beautiful."

Clara had professed herself not quite brave enough for a dye job, but she'd given the stylist free rein as far as cut and style. Gone was the mousy, nondescript mass of hair tied back in an indifferent bun. It had been replaced by a chic bob styled into fashionable marcelled curls, a look favored by all the biggest film stars. The curls showed off the glossy shine of her hair, which now framed her face most flatteringly.

"The back of my neck will get cold," Clara muttered. "Have I made a mistake? Oh, I'm afraid to look."

She looked so adorably worried that Addie wished she could lean down and kiss her nose, but she didn't dare in the middle of the salon. "First of all, if your neck does get cold, I'll make you a nice warm scarf to keep it warm. Secondly, it's just hair. If you don't like the way it looks now, it'll grow back. And thirdly, look at yourself."

Addie swiveled the chair back toward the mirror so Clara could see. Her mouth fell open into a perfect round O.

"Oh my," she said quietly. She leaned forward, watching her reflection as if she expected it not to move with her. "Is that really me?"

"Of course it's you, silly." Addie allowed herself to rest her chin on Clara's shoulder. That could be passed off as an affectionate gesture between close friends.

"You do look lovely, miss," the stylist said. "You have excellent bone structure for that type of flapper look. I wish I could pull it off half so well."

"I can't believe it," Clara said, still staring at herself.

She turned her head as if to admire herself from different angles. A smile slowly overtook her face, and Addie thought the stylist was wrong. Clara didn't look merely lovely; she looked radiant. For some reason, the sight sent a pang through Addie's chest. Clara shouldn't need a haircut or compliments to feel beautiful, but she hadn't had a lot of encouragement to feel good about herself until recently. Addie was taken aback by how genuinely fond she was becoming of Clara. She wanted Clara to be happy because she cared about her, not just because her own position relied on Clara being content.

Clara winced at the twelve dollar cost but handed it over along with a generous tip. Addie knew she was still getting used to having money to spend, especially on herself. She had only been a wealthy woman for a few weeks, not nearly enough time to break the habit of a lifetime of pinching pennies. Addie felt similarly whenever she was in between benefactors, but she had enough experience of being able to buy whatever she wanted that it was an easier adjustment for her.

Their next stop was a chic department store where they spent over an hour outfitting themselves with the newest designs. "I know it sounds silly, but none of my old clothes go with my new hair," Clara said as if she was trying to convince herself of the necessity.

"You don't have to justify it," Addie assured her.

"I suppose you're right," Clara said uneasily. "I still feel a bit guilty about it, but I suppose that will fade with time."

Addie nodded encouragingly. What was the point of being wealthy if not to enjoy it? She certainly wouldn't be feeling such qualms if she were in Clara's shoes. She wouldn't be so tacky as to outright ask Clara to buy her things, but she wasn't above dropping a few hints about some of the nicer items for sale. "Shall we walk to the apartment viewing or take the streetcar?" she asked.

Clara checked her watch. "I didn't realize how late it had gotten. Let's take a cab so we don't miss our appointment."

❖

"It's perfect," Clara said, clapping her hands in glee.

The apartment looked even better in person than it had in the *Globe* listing she and Addie had read and reread obsessively on the ship. Addie beamed and nodded, to Clara's relief. Even though it was her money, she wanted Addie to love it just as much as she did. It was to be their home together, after all. She might be the one with the money, but she liked to think that in all other ways, the two of them were on equal footing. She hoped Addie felt the same.

She couldn't sign the lease fast enough. Maybe she ought to have visited a few more places, but this one felt like home as soon as the building manager welcomed them into the lobby. Even at the exorbitant price of one hundred and fifty dollars a month, it was worth every penny. It was on the top floor of Boston's newest Art Deco building with all the latest features: a restaurant, a hair salon off the lobby, and even an elevator, staffed around the clock. The living room got plenty of light and was large enough for her to use one end of it for a studio. The windows went nearly floor to ceiling, and the tenth-floor views of the city were spectacular.

Since she owned no furniture, she and Addie went on another shopping spree before moving in. Never in her wildest dreams could she have imagined this would be her life someday. It probably wasn't the future her grandfather had envisioned for her when he left her his estate, but it was hers to do with as she pleased.

Her mother wasn't crazy about the modern apartment but grudgingly admitted it would be satisfactory until she found a husband and started a family. She and Addie studiously avoided each other's eyes until her family left, and they could laugh about it in private. It was a shame she'd disappoint her mother by remaining seemingly single, but she was too happy in her new life to mind too much.

Addie kept her things in the little second bedroom for the sake of appearances when Clara's family came over but spent every night in Clara's bed. The novelty of Addie being next to her each morning when she woke didn't grow old. She had promised to tell Addie if she got tired of her, but she didn't think that would ever happen. Every day felt more exciting with Addie by her side, the world full of endless possibilities instead of the staid predictability of her old life.

It took time for her to adjust to her newfound wealth, and she frequently found herself defaulting to the thrifty practices her parents had ingrained in her. She delighted in surprising Addie with gifts but was reluctant to spend much on herself. She didn't even notice the habit until Addie pointed it out to her.

"Really, you spoil me," Addie said, beaming as she petted the mink coat Clara had given her. "And when you were darning your stockings last night instead of buying new ones."

"I like you to have nice things," Clara said with a shrug. "Those stockings were easily mended. It would have been frivolous to throw them away. This is brand new."

"Don't go wasting all your money on me," Addie scolded.

Clara smiled and waved off her concern. She could see how much Addie loved the gift, and all she wanted was to make her smile like that again.

Even with the splurges of the apartment and the things she bought for Addie, she wasn't worried. The financial advisor she'd consulted assured her that her current spending was well within her limits, and if she was willing to take a chance on the stock market, he was certain he could turn the estate into a veritable fortune.

She intended to, but it would involve several boring trips to the bank, and there was always something more fun to do. For now, she was content leaving most of the money in the treasury bonds her grandfather had left her and spending most of her time with Addie.

CHAPTER FIFTEEN

Although she hadn't been there before, Addie quickly grew to like living in Boston. Clara took great pains to make sure she was happy, giving her free rein over most of the apartment decor and a charge account at Filene's Department Store.

Addie bought herself a few nice things here and there but found herself feeling guilty every time she gave the store clerk Clara's account number for a new handbag or piece of jewelry. It was nothing she hadn't gleefully done many times before with half a dozen previous lovers, but with Clara, it felt uncomfortable, even wrong.

Of course, none of her other lovers had looked at her with stars in their eyes the way that Clara did or removed her clothes to draw tender and flattering portraits of her before making love to her. Doubtlessly, Clara's infatuation with her wouldn't last long, but she was clearly still in the throes of it. It would be wise to accumulate as much money for herself as she could before Clara inevitably tired of her.

Sometimes, Addie wondered if Eva would have grown sick of her too, had she lived. Eva had loved her in a way no other woman had before or since, but in her darkest moments, Addie felt sure it would have fizzled out just like the rest. She was someone to be shown off and pampered for a few months before moving on, not a lifelong love.

The smart course of action would have been to set aside as much cash and luxury goods as she could get her hands on. She had her own future to think of. Certainly, no one else was going to do it. Eva had talked about leaving Addie an allowance in her will but had never gotten around to it. It had always seemed like there would be endless time to take care of boring things like wills, but Eva's illness had struck so quickly and viciously. Suddenly, time was in desperately short supply.

Addie wondered if she could get Clara to leave her a bequest or settle a sum of money on her before they went their separate ways. It didn't have to be much, just enough to live on. She was a simple person at heart. All she wanted was a home of her own where she wasn't answerable to anyone. She'd rather have that than a hundred fur coats. It didn't seem like so much to ask.

The problem was that the more time she spent with Clara, the less she wanted to think about the future after their relationship was over. Sometimes, she even let herself imagine them growing old together, Clara with her art, Addie with her books and records and handicrafts. It was a quiet life, maybe not terribly thrilling to an outside observer, but its allure was palpable to her. It wasn't all that different from the life she'd always dreamed of, but the idea of being alone didn't hold the same appeal it once had. She had a hard time picturing being this happy without Clara. Being with Clara felt somehow both safe and exciting at the same time.

She knew it couldn't last. If Clara ever found out the truth or even suspected there had been anything calculating in her actions, it would all come crumbling down. Even more likely, Clara *would* tire of her and want to move on. She had to face the fact that that would someday happen, and yet, she didn't want to. Ignoring facts didn't make them not true, but their life together made her too happy to worry about that yet.

When the weather was nice, they went for long walks around the city, scoping out new places for Clara to draw and paint. She spent hours drawing the ducks in the Public Garden while Addie sat nearby knitting, her needles clicking as she people-watched. Other times, she read, then summarized her current novel or magazine for Clara as they walked home.

Clara found herself more passionate than ever about her art. She seemed to have a bottomless font of ideas pouring out of her, eager to be expressed. She could easily spend hours on a single sketch, losing all sense of time or awareness of her surroundings. Once, she emerged from a particularly focused drawing session to find an angry goose hissing at her. Addie hurried over to shepherd her to safety, fending off the aggressive bird with her umbrella as they fled.

"How could you possibly not have noticed it?" Addie asked incredulously once she had finally stopped laughing.

Clara shrugged, trying to figure out how to explain. "I don't know. When I'm like that, it's like…a radio tuned to static or something. There's no input from the outside world at all."

"It's a good thing I came back when I did to rescue you."

"You were very heroic," Clara said. "You looked like a brave knight with your trusty lance."

Addie laughed, then handed Clara her umbrella. "I haven't been properly knighted yet."

"Kneel," Clara said imperiously. Addie did so, both of them laughing as Clara tapped each of her shoulders with the umbrella. "I dub thee Lady Adeline of Chicago, brave defender of hapless artists. Arise."

A man and woman about their age stared as Addie stood, still giggling. Clara gave them a hard stare until she recognized the man as her cousin.

"Hello, Harry," she called, waving. She realized she was still holding Addie's umbrella and lowered her arm hurriedly.

He started to turn away without acknowledging her, but the woman beside him tugged on his arm, and he was forced to wait as Clara and Addie approached.

"Hello, Cousin Clara," he said stiffly, looking at a point slightly over her left shoulder. His companion cleared her throat pointedly. "This is Miss Julia Sullivan. My fiancée."

Clara introduced herself and Addie to Julia since Harry didn't. He looked like he wanted to leave, but Julia had engaged Addie in a conversation about knitting.

"Come along, dear," he said, his hand on her elbow.

She shook him off. "Not just yet, I'm in the middle of a conversation."

"Julia. Now," he snapped.

She gave him an icy glare, and he practically wilted. She and Addie finished their discussion of the best techniques for working with double-pointed knitting needles while Harry and Clara waited in silence, Harry shifting awkwardly from foot to foot. Clara was pleased to see that Julia was no shrinking violet. Between Harry's outsized ego and Matilda's overbearing personality, Clara had worried about Julia holding her own. Clearly, she had no need to worry.

"She wasn't at all what I expected," Addie said as they left. "Harry was, though."

Clara laughed. "Yes, I'm surprised at how much I liked her. I wonder what she sees in him."

"Maybe he has hidden depths underneath the layers of self-importance," Addie mused.

"For her sake, I hope so," Clara said.

"Look, she gave me her card. She asked if we'd visit with her once the baby is born and keep her company." Addie showed Clara Julia's card, which was embossed and printed on creamy white cardstock.

"She's probably desperate to spend time with anyone other than Harry and Matilda."

"I'm glad we don't have that struggle," Addie said, smiling at her in a way that sent butterflies racing in her stomach. "There's no one I'd rather spend my days with. Or my nights, for that matter."

"Don't be a sap," Clara chided, but she could feel the heat rising in her cheeks.

She had thought about telling Addie that she loved her, but she kept putting it off. Addie was still recovering from losing Eva and might not be ready to be loved again. Clara didn't want to overwhelm her in her healing process. Besides, they hadn't known each other all that long. It was better to keep her feelings to herself for now.

CHAPTER SIXTEEN

Although most evenings, Clara would have been content to stay in listening to records or the radio, she worried that Addie would get bored with just her for company. The last thing she wanted was for Addie to feel trapped with her just because she had no other options. Clara knew too well what that had felt like, always having to make nice to Aunt Matilda before she got her inheritance. Addie deserved to have more of a social circle than just Clara. Once or twice a week, they went to a gin joint in the neighborhood. The first time, Clara was shocked both at how nice it was and how little the proprietors bothered trying to hide what it was.

"Not what you expected, is it?" Addie asked.

Clara shook her head, admiring the tuxedo-clad jazz band and the well-heeled patrons. "I thought it would be…dirtier."

Addie threw her head back and laughed. "There are certainly places like that, but I don't think either of us would enjoy them. Besides, I asked around to make sure this one would be safe. The head of the Prohibition squad for the police department drinks here on most of his nights off, so it never gets raided."

"That seems rather hypocritical, doesn't it? For the people who are supposed to be enforcing the law to flout it and get special privileges for their friends?"

"I suppose," Addie said with a nonchalant shrug. "It's just the way the world works, though. We might as well take advantage of it. Would you rather be somewhere else where we'd have to worry about cops showing up?"

"No, of course not."

"Well then, what's the problem? You can't change it, so there's no point in trying."

Neither the hypocrisy nor Addie's defeatist attitude about it sat right with Clara, but she didn't want to get into an argument. As she took a sip of her sidecar cocktail, a blond man in a pinstripe suit sidled up to their table.

"Good evening, ladies," he said, his words slurring slightly. "Would you care to dance?"

His eyes were fixed on Addie, and Clara felt as invisible as she used to wish she was back in high school.

"No thank you," Addie said, barely glancing at him. She ran her foot up Clara's shin under the table reassuringly.

"C'mon," he wheedled. "You're the best-looking girl in this place. Ditch your pal and come have some fun."

"I said no. We're in the middle of a conversation, and you're interrupting," Addie said coldly.

He lurched away, muttering something that Clara was just as glad she couldn't hear. She was certain it was none too flattering or polite.

"How very annoying," Addie said. She sounded bored, as if it was a commonplace occurrence for her. Clara supposed it probably was.

"I wish we could go somewhere where that wouldn't happen," Clara said wistfully. She trusted that Addie had no interest in the men who approached her, but it bothered her that she couldn't do anything to indicate that they were an item, and Addie wasn't available.

Addie's face brightened. "As a matter of fact, there probably is somewhere like that. Give me a few days to ask around."

A week later, they ventured out of their neighborhood to a nondescript doorway in a nondescript street where Addie muttered a password as Clara looked around furtively to make sure they weren't being watched. They could hear a series of locks being undone before the door finally swung open just long enough for them to slip inside.

"Welcome to Rosie's," the man at the door said. His voice was oddly high-pitched, and Clara did a double take when she looked closer and realized he was actually a woman. Addie looked unfazed, and Clara tried not to stare.

They descended a flight of stairs into the main area of Rosie's, where there were plenty of other things to indicate that it wasn't like any place she had been before. She tensed when Addie laced their fingers together, but she needn't have worried.

Like the door attendant, the bartender was wearing a men's suit. She gave Addie an admiring look that made Clara want to slap her. At the same time, she felt a strange sort of delight that the woman felt comfortable so openly expressing her interest in another woman.

"You new?" the bartender asked when they approached. She was short and stocky, her eyes an even more vivid blue than Addie's. She had shed her suit jacket and rolled up the sleeves of her buttoned shirt to reveal a tattoo curling up her lower arm. Clara had never seen anyone with tattoos aside from sailors or at the circus.

They nodded and introduced themselves.

"I'm Rosie. First drink's on the house. What'll it be? I'd go with gin if I were you. My usual whiskey source went dry this month, and the new stuff isn't any good."

"We appreciate the warning," Addie said drily. "I'll have a gin rickey, then. Clarabella?"

"The same," Clara said.

Rosie was still looking at Addie hungrily, but her eyes flicked to Clara at the pet name. To drive the point home, Clara slid her arm around Addie's waist possessively and kissed her cheek.

"Can't blame me for trying," Rosie said, laughing. She accepted her defeat with good grace, Clara had to give her that. "Hold on to your girl there, she's a looker."

"I'm right here," Addie said indignantly, but even in the dim lighting, Clara could see she was blushing. Her reaction was a far cry from her utter disdain for the man who'd asked her to dance at the other club.

"Here are your drinks. Enjoy yourselves, you hear? And if anyone gives you any trouble, call me right over. I don't stand for any nonsense here. That's not just for show." Rosie pointed grimly at a shotgun mounted on the wall behind the bar.

Clara hadn't noticed it before, and the sight sent a shiver down her spine. She wondered what sort of "nonsense" Rosie needed it for. Hopefully, it wouldn't be necessary tonight, at any rate.

They took their drinks and found a vacant table near the back of the long, narrow room, right next to the dance floor. The vibe was worlds apart from their regular speakeasy. The lighting was dim, perhaps to avoid attracting attention from outside. Instead of a live band, a phonograph in the corner was blaring out a Jelly Roll Morton record.

Clara scanned the crowd of dancers, her mouth falling open as she realized how many were pairs of women or men. They laughed as they danced, holding each other openly, joy evident in their faces. She had never imagined a place of such freedom. Despite everything she'd seen on her European adventure, she thought this was the most magical experience of her life so far. The crowd went blurry, and she realized she was tearing up.

Addie watched her dab at her eyes, a tender smile on her face. "What do you think?"

"It's…it's beautiful," she said quietly.

The words didn't do justice to what she was feeling, but Addie seemed to understand. She brought Clara's hand to her mouth and kissed it, then tugged her to her feet. "Dance with me."

Clara didn't think much of her dancing skills normally, but in Addie's arms, she felt as graceful as a ballerina. Addie danced the gentleman's role, twirling her and dipping her with ease. She had obviously done it before, and Clara was grateful that she herself wasn't having to adjust to a whole new style of dance when she wasn't good at it to begin with.

They danced until their feet ached and they were gasping for breath, then sat and rested and danced some more. Sometimes, a shadow crossed Addie's face when they stopped. Whenever it did, she would pull Clara to her feet and back out onto the dance floor, even if they'd only been sitting for a minute. Clara wanted to ask about it, but she was having such a nice time that she hated to spoil it. It might have been selfish, but she wanted to enjoy the evening and save an emotional conversation for another day.

Finally, they staggered up the stairs where the doorwoman made them wait until she'd checked that the coast was clear before letting them out. Clara blinked against the sudden intrusion of light outside; the sun was starting to rise. They had quite literally danced the night away.

They found a cab a few blocks away, their sore feet throbbing as they rode home in companionable silence. Clara let her head fall onto

Addie's shoulder, dozing until they reached home. Once they got inside their apartment, though, she felt as energized as if she'd just been wired for electricity.

"That was magical," she said, twirling around in the entryway.

Addie winced as she pulled off her shoes, then gave a tired smile. "I'm glad you had such a nice time."

Guiltily, Clara remembered the moments when she had ignored Addie looking unhappy. "Is everything all right? Sometimes tonight, you looked…sad."

Addie paused in removing her stockings. "I'm fine," she said, not fully meeting Clara's eyes. "I'm just tired, and my feet hurt."

Clara wanted to take her at her word, but the explanation didn't quite ring true. Somehow, she knew Addie was holding something back. "I wish you'd talk to me," she blurted. "I know that wasn't all. Why won't you tell me what's wrong?"

Addie looked shocked at her outburst. "There's nothing wrong, really. Wouldn't you rather just go to bed?"

"I don't believe you. If you're not comfortable telling me, that's all right, but don't lie to me."

After a long pause, Addie said, "Fine. I'd rather not talk about it. It's nothing about you, if that helps."

"It does," Clara said, nodding. "I hope someday, you'll feel you can trust me with it, but I'll leave you be until then." She kept her word and didn't pry any more, even when she heard Addie crying in the bathroom after she no doubt thought Clara had fallen asleep.

Addie had let her guard down, allowing Clara to see the mix of emotions she'd felt about being at Rosie's. Memories of many similar evenings she'd spent with Eva had come rushing back, threatening to overwhelm her with grief and guilt in equal measure.

They'd never talked about what would happen once Eva was gone, but surely, she would have wanted Addie to find love again. That didn't make her feel any less guilty, though. Being with Clara made her happier than she ever would have anticipated, but she couldn't shake the sense of disloyalty to Eva's memory.

Clara wouldn't want to hear about any of it, though. She knew

Addie as fun and lighthearted and undemanding. It would take longer for her to get tired of someone who never asked anything of her beyond a few gifts every now and then. However much Clara might insist she wanted Addie to be more open, no one really wanted to know about their partner's lost lover.

Rosie's became their regular haunt, despite the dingy interior and low quality liquor. Addie was hesitant to go back after her emotional reaction the first time, but Clara was so eager that she acquiesced. It was obvious how much more Clara liked it than the nicer speakeasy, and Addie was a sucker for making her smile. They befriended some of the other regulars, as well as Rosie herself. She still flirted with Addie sometimes but never so outrageously that Clara got offended.

"I never knew there were so many of us," Clara said one night, humming off-key and bouncing along in her seat to the Duke Ellington tune that was blaring from the phonograph.

Addie nodded, smiling at how Clara seemed unaware of her own dancing. Whatever Rosie had gotten her hands on this week tasted like a higher proof than usual, and Clara was several cocktails in. The combination of the inheritance, Addie's attention, and finding this community had done wonders for Clara's confidence.

"Are you quite all right?" she asked, seeing that Clara was now squinting at a dark corner of the bar. Maybe the drinks were even stronger than she thought, and she needed to cut Clara off for her own well-being.

"Is that…Gerald, is that you?" Clara said, ignoring Addie completely and standing.

A young man seated at a table in the corner Clara had been staring at jumped up and started toward the exit. Unfortunately for him, he had to pass their table to reach it.

"Gerald? Gerald, it's me, Clara Cooper. Willoughby High, class of 1922. Do you remember me?"

"I…I…I must go, excuse me," he muttered. He pushed past, not looking at either of them and practically ran to the door.

Addie put a hand on Clara's arm to stop her from going after him. "Let him go."

"But why wouldn't he speak to me? He was one of the only nice ones," Clara said sadly.

"Think about where we are," Addie said. "I'm sure he feels awkward about anyone he knows seeing him in here."

"But he saw me too," Clara said. "It isn't as if I could tell anyone without revealing the same thing about myself."

"I'm sure that didn't even occur to him. People are often irrational about such things. The first time I saw someone I knew from home in similar circumstances, I don't think either of us could think of anything but panic at the idea of being found out."

"It's awful, isn't it." Clara visibly wilted, her good mood gone.

Addie wished she'd toughen up. The world was a cruel and uncaring place, and it was past time Clara understood that. Addie ought to let her figure it out for herself, but it pained her to see Clara sad for even a moment.

She would have to come up with some way of cheering Clara up, especially since her birthday was only a few days away. Fortunately, she had hit upon the perfect gift idea.

CHAPTER SEVENTEEN

"Happy birthday," Addie said. She lifted the cloth covering off the gift with a flourish.

Clara gasped as the birdcage underneath was revealed. Its occupant, a bright green bird, tilted its head at her quizzically and chirped. Her heart melted. "Hello, little fellow."

"Do you like him?" Addie asked, watching her intently. "I knew it was risky, buying you an animal when we hadn't talked about it, but I saw him in the pet shop, and it seemed like the perfect gift. He's a… let's see…" She checked the pamphlet she'd produced from behind the cage "A green-cheeked conure, which is a sort of parakeet. He's very social and can live for up to thirty years, so if you don't want the responsibility, I can take him back."

"Don't you dare take him away from me," Clara said indignantly. She moved closer to admire her new friend up close. True to his name, although the feathers of his head were gray and black, his cheeks looked like he was wearing bright green rouge. His wing feathers ranged from green to deep blue, and some of his tail feathers were a lovely contrasting red.

"They offered to clip his wings before I brought him home, but I wasn't sure you'd want that," Addie said. "We can bring him back for that if you'd like."

Clara was aghast. "No! The very idea. It seems cruel, taking flight away from him."

"In that case, we'll just have to be very careful that he never gets outside when he's out of his cage," Addie said.

Clara nodded, watching him look around with bright, intelligent eyes.

"What are you going to call him?" Addie asked.

Clara pondered the question, looking around the room for inspiration. Her eyes landed on Addie's bookshelf, and she walked over to it. Scanning the titles, she considered and discarded a number of options before selecting a few of her favorite characters.

"What do you think, little fellow?" she asked the bird. "Are you a Queequeg? No, that doesn't suit you. How about Monsieur Poirot? That's too long to say every day…"

Addie was watching her, an indeterminate expression on her face.

"What?" Clara asked defensively. She probably sounded ridiculous, and Addie was trying not to laugh at her.

"I love you," Addie said.

Clara stared at her, her heart speeding up. They had never spoken those words aloud, despite living together for several months now.

"It's all right if you don't feel the same," Addie said nervously, and Clara realized she had been silent for far too long.

"No, I do. I…I love you too," she said, relishing the shy smile that spread across Addie's face. She wanted to say it over and over again but didn't want to scare Addie off with the force of her affection. She looked at her bird again instead.

She hit upon the perfect name for him. "I think I'll call you Pip."

"*Great Expectations*?" Addie asked, moving to stand beside her.

Clara nodded. "Thankfully, I had a happier upbringing than Dickens's Pip, but I do relate to suddenly inheriting a fortune."

"I guess that makes me Estella," Addie said. "Although I'm sure I could do a good Miss Havisham impression if I put my mind to it."

Clara giggled at the thought. "I like to think that she put that old wedding dress on whenever people came over so that people would stop pestering her about getting married, and the rest of the time, she was having the time of her life."

"It's a good cover story," Addie agreed.

"Maybe that would work on my mother," Clara said ruefully.

"She means well," Addie said soothingly.

"I know she does, but it doesn't make it any less aggravating when she pesters me about how much happier I'll be once I find a husband. I wish I could tell her the truth."

Addie looked alarmed. "Don't do that."

"I'm not going to," Clara assured her. "But I'm already happier than I've ever been in my life, and I want her to know that. I have you, what more could I possibly need?"

Addie put an arm around her and leaned her head on Clara's shoulder. "It's hard to accept that most people can't understand us. Hopefully, she knows how happy you are, at least in some unconscious way."

Clara hoped Addie was right. She wasn't about to give up the life of her dreams now that she'd achieved it, but she still wanted to please her family. She wasn't going to worry about that tonight, though. She had more important things to think about, like being in love.

Addie feigned a headache and spent the night in her "official" bedroom on the other side of the apartment. Being near Clara tonight felt dangerous, with her heart exposed and raw as it was. Her stupid mouth had gotten ahead of her brain and blurted out feelings she would rather have kept private.

Even worse than her horror at having admitted her love for Clara was the long pause when Clara had simply stood there in the aftermath. It had probably only been a few seconds, but Addie's anxious mind had run through a dozen possibilities in that time. Clara didn't love her back and was trying to figure out the kindest way to let her down gently. Clara didn't love her back and was worried Addie would cling on and refuse to leave.

Instead, most terrifyingly of all, Clara reciprocated her feelings. This was perhaps the worst possible outcome and the one most likely to lead to one or both of them getting hurt. She didn't want to love Clara. Everyone she ever loved had left her in one way or another.

Clara loving her back didn't help matters, either. She wanted to be able to excise herself cleanly from the relationship if it came to that. It would be far easier if Clara thought of her as merely a bit of fun she could buy off when she grew tired of her. It was hard to imagine Clara doing such a thing. Impossible, really. But Addie hadn't lasted this long by trusting too much in anyone's good nature. However kind Clara was, she surely had a tipping point just like anyone else. Addie would delay that as long as she could, of course. She had a good thing here, and it would be foolish to mess it up because of something as valueless as feelings.

To that end, she did all the things she'd learned about the hard way from past relationships. She made sure she woke before Clara every morning to do her face. Clara had not yet seen her without makeup, and she needed to keep it that way for as long as possible. She elided the details of her past whenever it came up. A mysterious orphan from urban Chicago was a lot more alluring than the truth. As long as she kept one step ahead of Clara, there was no reason she should ever find out.

CHAPTER EIGHTEEN

A re you sure you won't come with me?"

Addie raised her eyebrows, shuddering. "Much as I'd enjoy seeing Matilda's reaction to my showing up uninvited, I think I'll pass, thanks."

"You can't blame me for trying. It's not like I'm eager to go either," Clara said with a smile. She pulled her gloves on and checked the angle of her borrowed hat in the mirror, a brimmed cloche like the one Greta Garbo had worn in *Anna Christie*. She had bought it for Addie, who read both fashion and movie magazines with enthusiasm. Personally, she thought it looked far better on Addie than on Garbo, but Addie had brushed off the compliment and called her a flatterer and a shameless flirt when she'd said so.

She lingered as long as she could, but finally, Addie shepherded her toward the door, admonishing her not to be late, or she'd never hear the end of it.

Luck was on Clara's side, and her taxi pulled up at the Copley Plaza just as her mother stepped out of her own cab. It always felt better to go into an encounter with Aunt Matilda with an ally at her side.

"It shouldn't take Matilda to get us together," her mother chided, pulling her into a hug. "We're only fifteen miles away, and we haven't seen you in nearly a month."

"I know, and I'm sorry about that. Time really does fly by," Clara said, tucking her arm through her mother's as a doorman led them inside.

"It's all right. We miss you, that's all. You and Addie should come stay for the weekend. I'm glad you girls are having fun in the city. You look lovely, by the way. Is that a new hat?"

Matilda's smile was more of a grimace when she spotted them approaching her table in the tea room. She still hadn't forgiven Clara for the change in Henry Cooper's will, even though she and Harry had plenty of money of their own. Clara supposed it was more the principle of the thing. She and Harry were the wealthy and upstanding branch of the Coopers, while Clara and her family were the starving artists. They were on much more equal footing now, and clearly, Matilda didn't like it one bit.

"Anne, Clara," she said in greeting. "You've met Julia?"

They said hello to Julia, Harry's new wife. She stayed seated, her pregnancy shielded by the table.

"It's nice to see you again, Cousin Clara," Julia said. "How is your companion?"

"*Tuh*," Matilda said before Clara could answer. "It's an outrage that that woman is still in our lives. It's a good thing that Henry left the family silver to Harry, or it would probably be in pawn shops all over Boston by now."

Clara bristled, but her mother gave her a quelling look to indicate that she would handle it. "We've had nothing but good experiences with Miss Barnes."

"I know her type. They're always crafty when they know there's a family fortune to be exploited," Matilda said, with a sideways glance at her daughter-in-law.

Julia ignored the obvious insult and smiled at Matilda sweetly, which was more than Clara could have managed in her shoes. She was as gracious as Matilda was boorish, and Clara genuinely enjoyed her company.

Toward the end of luncheon, Matilda left them to go to the powder room, and Clara seized the opportunity.

"I have to know, what on earth are you doing with Harry?" she asked.

Her mother gasped in horror at her bluntness. "*Clara.*"

"It's fine," Julia said, waving off the disapproval. "To tell you the truth, I felt rather sorry for him. I think he's got potential, but he's never had to prove himself or earn anything in his life. He only got his clerkship because Father used to play golf with your grandfather. He needs someone who pushes him to be better instead of being constantly coddled like he always has been."

"I commend you for your sense of charity," Clara said, grinning. Her mother looked torn between being scandalized and amused.

Julia laughed. "I do hope you and Addie will come visit sometime. I'd love to get to know you both better. You as well, Mrs. Cooper."

Matilda returned, complaining about the slowness of the waitstaff in bringing the check. Clara would have loved to see her aunt's reaction to Julia's perception of Harry, which couldn't have been more different than hers. In the interest of keeping the peace, she said nothing. Julia was facing an uphill battle already. Clara certainly wasn't going to make it any harder for her.

She was relieved to be going home to Addie, who she loved and respected and who didn't come with an awful mother-in-law. Hopefully Julia would be able to find some measure of happiness with Harry, even if the very idea filled Clara with horror. She couldn't imagine what her own life might have become if it weren't for her inheritance. A situation like Julia's, shackled to a wealthy husband, would have been the best she could realistically have hoped for. Instead, she got to live the life of her dreams with Addie. It felt almost unfair for one person to have so much good fortune.

❖

Clara's reward for making it through luncheon with Matilda was a particularly enjoyable evening at Rosie's with Addie. It was pouring rain as they dashed down the block from where their cab had dropped them, their shoes soaked by the time they reached the unmarked door. They always gave an address a block or two away so as not to attract any undue attention to the building.

The rain had finally stopped by the time they left Rosie's, so they decided to walk home to get some fresh air instead of hailing a cab. After dancing all evening, it felt oppressive not to be able to hold Addie's hand as they walked, but Clara knew it was safer not to. She looped her arm through Addie's instead, enjoying the warmth of their bodies near each other. There was a chill in the air, indicating that summer was well and truly over.

Clara's feet were aching from the long walk in her dancing shoes, and she was relieved when they turned onto their street. She was so focused on getting home that she collided with a man emerging from the hotel a block away from their building.

"Watch it," he said sharply.

"I'm sorry," she said, embarrassed.

Usually, Addie would step in and smooth things over in situations like this. Between her striking good looks and pleasant manner, she always seemed to make unpleasant problems disappear. To Clara's surprise, however, Addie wasn't even looking at her or the man she'd bumped into. Instead, she was leaning away from Clara, her face turned to the side and her hat pulled down low.

"That's all right," the man grumbled.

Clara looked back at him. She had nearly forgotten him, so preoccupied was she with Addie's odd behavior.

"Let's go," Addie muttered, tugging on Clara's arm.

Clara allowed Addie to lead her away from the man. They were a few steps away when he called out after them:

"Hey, wait a minute."

Clara turned and saw him starting toward them, a puzzled look on his face.

"You there," he said, looking past her at Addie.

Addie didn't look back, but Clara could feel her stiffen. Clara was baffled by her visceral reaction to the stranger, but it was clear that she was terrified.

"Wait," he called again.

Addie sped up, now fully dragging Clara by the arm. "Come on," she said desperately. "We need to get away from that man."

They had almost reached the refuge of the lobby, with its doorman and elevator attendants on hand to fend off the pursuing stranger, when he caught up with them. Addie tried to wriggle free, but he had her trapped with a firm grip on her shoulders.

"What do you want with her?" Clara cried, swinging her handbag into his shoulder. It might as well have been a fly trying to knock over a horse for all the good it did. She looked around for someone to intervene, but the sidewalk was deserted.

"A man has a right to talk to his own sister," he snapped, his eyes fixed on Addie.

Clara froze as the meaning of his words sank in. "You've mistaken her for somebody else. All her family is dead."

"So that's the story you've gone with," he said. "We might as well be, for all you care. Taking off in the middle of the night, not so much as a note letting us know you're still alive."

"I did write," Addie said indignantly. "Once I got to Kansas City, I sent Ma a letter. She wrote *refused* and sent it back unopened, so I know she got it, even if she didn't read it. I recognized her handwriting."

"Oh. She didn't tell us that." He looked flummoxed by her words but not for long. "Well…you also stole the money they were saving for a new mule."

"That's true." Addie looked at him steadily. "That was wrong, and I shouldn't have done it. I mailed her a check a few years ago, but she sent that back too. It was forty-two dollars and eighty cents, if I recall correctly. Shall we round it up to fifty to make up for the length of time?" She pulled a wad of bills out of her purse, selected a few, and held them out. He eyed the money suspiciously, then snatched it out of her hand as if she might take it away if he was too slow. He counted it out, a stony expression on his face. Other than his blue eyes, he didn't bear much resemblance to Addie.

"What are you doing in Boston, anyway?" Addie asked.

He paused for so long that Clara wondered if he was going to answer. Finally, he folded the money, tucked it into the inside pocket of his overcoat, and said, "Meeting. I'm on the board of the Agricultural Bank of Kansas. We're being bought out by some big bank up here."

"Clearly, you've done well enough for yourself," Addie said coolly.

"As have you. That felt like real fur. It must have cost what, five, six hundred dollars? What are you, a wealthy widow?" He looked between Addie and Clara, his expression turning stormy. "No, not a widow. A kept woman. *Her* kept woman."

He jabbed a finger in Clara's direction, and she could feel the disgust radiating off him. It chilled her in a way the night air couldn't. Even though intellectually, she knew there were plenty of people who would disapprove, she was still shocked by the level of revulsion in his face. She couldn't imagine even Aunt Matilda looking at her like that. How horrible it must have been for Addie to grow up surrounded by people who so obviously despised her. "Take your money and go," she snapped, tucking her arm through Addie's protectively.

Neither she nor Addie spoke as they walked the short distance to their building. Clara used the time to mull over everything she'd heard. Now that the immediate sense of danger had passed, things weren't adding up right. She realized Addie had been lying to her. She wasn't from Chicago at all. Clara thought back to the times she'd tried to get Addie to talk more about her past. Now that she was paying attention, she realized that Addie always managed to dodge or deflect such questions. What else had she lied about?

Curse my rotten luck. Why, of all the people from her past whom she might have run into, did it have to be Roger? If only she'd plucked up the courage to tell Clara about that part of her life before the story was being forced out of her.

Addie stared at her lap and fiddled with her handkerchief. Several times, she opened her mouth to speak, but the words wouldn't come. Pip fluttered over and landed on her shoulder, tilting his head worriedly. She gave him a tiny smile and finally met Clara's gaze.

"I'm from Kansas originally. I grew up on a farm outside of a town you've never heard of, only a few hundred people. You know how small towns are—if you stand out in any way, it makes you a target. I had this friend I was just crazy about. I thought she felt the same, and I tried to kiss her, but she told everyone."

The same bitterness she always felt when she thought of Christine flooded through her. No matter how deeply she buried the memories, she would never forget the humiliation or the fear of discovery.

"That was unkind of her," Clara said, sounding outraged. "What did she have to tell everyone else for?"

Addie smiled in spite of herself. Even though Clara was under-standably upset with her, she still instinctively rose to her defense. Clara really had the sweetest nature of anyone she'd ever met.

"My parents were furious. I didn't know what they were planning until my little sister Daisy told me they were going to try to have me committed."

Clara gasped. "Their own daughter, how horrible."

Addie squeezed her balled-up handkerchief, a lump forming in her throat. It was still painful to relive the memories, even all these years later. "I had to get away fast in the middle of the night. I stole the money like Roger said, and I ran. I lived in Kansas City and then Chicago until I met Eva, and she brought me to Europe."

She had skimmed over a lot, particularly the years in Kansas City and Chicago when she'd lived with other women before Eva came along, but Clara wouldn't want to hear about all that.

Clara frowned. "So your family is still alive, then."

Addie shook her head, the lump in her throat now making it difficult to speak. She fished her wallet out of her handbag. From the hidden interior compartment, she retrieved the *Topeka Daily Capital* clipping and handed it to Clara.

"'Town loses tenth of population in one week to Spanish flu,'" Clara read the headline aloud. Her eyes scanned quickly over the short article, which Addie could have recited by heart. "'The dead are as follows: James Abernathy, age forty-seven; Elizabeth Allston, age twenty-nine; Daisy Barnes, age eleven...' Oh, Addie."

"Less than a month after I left," Addie said dully, accepting the clipping back from Clara and returning it to its storage place. "I went to the library every day to check the papers from all across the state in case there was any news from home. I won't ever forget what it felt like to see that article for the first time. I'll never know for sure, of course, but I think...I think it was my fault."

"How could it have been your fault?"

"The school was closed because of the flu, so Daisy hardly ever went into town. One of my chores was going to the market when we needed something. After I left, she would have been the one to take that over. Where else could she have gotten sick?"

"You can't possibly know that," Clara said. "She might have gotten it from the milkman or something."

Addie chuckled in spite of her misery. "We didn't have milk delivered. We had our own cow."

"Oh, right. Somehow, I can't picture you milking a cow or hoeing a field."

"And I want to keep it that way. Some people have the idiotic idea that farming is idyllic or tranquil or pleasant, but it's not. It's mostly thankless work and frequently dirty and smelly. You'd never want to kiss me again." Assuming, that was, that Clara still wanted her around after discovering the deception. Hester Windermere certainly wouldn't have. Addie tried to remind herself that Clara wasn't like Hester or any of the other women she'd been with who didn't really care about her, but she didn't quite believe her own reassurances.

"I don't believe *that*," Clara said, a tiny smile on her lips. "Was there anything you liked about it?"

Addie considered, relaxing the slightest bit now that Clara didn't seem on the verge of breaking it off with her immediately. "Tending the animals, the goats especially. They all have their own personalities, you know."

"What about your least favorite?"

"Working in the fields," Addie said with a shudder. She didn't even have to think about it. "Always kneeling or bending over, getting sunburned, all that dirt under my fingernails…no, thank you."

"There's this whole part of your life that I knew nothing about," Clara said, looking serious again. "I'm glad I know now, but I have to say, it hurts that it took running into your brother for me to find out about it."

"I know. I regret it now," Addie said. Truthfully, she would have given anything to redo the afternoon and avoid meeting Roger entirely, but Clara wasn't to know that.

"But why didn't you tell me the truth?" There was genuine pain in Clara's voice.

"I thought about it, but it seemed so uncomfortable to bring up out of the blue," Addie said. "And then the longer it went on without you knowing, the more awkward it would have been."

"So you just…hoped I'd never find out?" Clara asked in disbelief.

Addie shrugged miserably. "I suppose so. Truly, it didn't even feel like I was lying. When I told you all of that on the ship, it felt like so long ago, like a different lifetime. I try not to dwell on that part of my life if I can help it. I'd just as soon not talk about either version of my past."

"You mean, the true version and the lies you told me?" Clara snapped.

"Clarabella!" Addie knew she didn't have the right to be outraged, but the bite in Clara's tone stung, and Pip cheeped angrily.

Clara stood her ground. "They *were* lies, even if you didn't intend it as some grand deception."

"I never meant to hurt you."

"But you did," Clara said. "We're supposed to be a team, aren't we? A partnership? Whatever happened to us against the world? How can we be a team when I don't even know who you really are, when you don't trust me?"

Addie shook her head. Clara might think she wanted that, but that was only her naivety speaking. She had no idea what she was asking.

"Is there anything else you haven't told me?" Clara said dully. "Are you a German spy? Do you have a hidden past as a showgirl? Are you secretly married?"

Addie swallowed hard. If she was going to tell Clara that she'd known about her inheritance all along, it was now or never. But Clara was already having trouble absorbing what she'd found out tonight, and if Addie told her that part too, it might be too much. She couldn't bear Clara being even more upset with her than she was now.

CHAPTER NINETEEN

Clara was rattled by how thoroughly Addie had deceived her. It was weeks until she felt like she could trust her again. If they hadn't had the chance meeting with Roger Barnes, years might have passed before Clara had found out about Addie's family. Assuming, that was, if she ever did. Addie seemed sorrier at having been caught in a lie than about the lying itself.

Clara found herself scrutinizing everything she could remember Addie ever saying about herself or her life before they'd met. She couldn't think of any other obvious falsehoods. She had given Addie the chance to come clean about any other dishonesty, but clearly, she was not the best judge of when Addie was lying.

Addie seemed to sense the gulf growing between them. She was more attentive than ever, constantly bringing Clara cookies or cups of coffee while she was painting. It reached the point of being annoying rather than solicitous. Finally, she lost her temper.

"Would you stop interrupting me and just leave me alone?" she snapped as Addie came into the living room for the fifth time that morning bearing a tray laden with lemonade and petits fours.

Clara was on her umpteenth attempt at a portrait of Pip, agonizing over getting the colors of his feathers just right. He was being good about posing as long as she bribed him every now and then with peanuts, but at the sound of her raised voice, he took flight and fluttered to Addie's shoulder instead.

Addie looked stricken. She turned and left the room, Pip riding on her shoulder. Clara could hear the tray clattering somewhere, then a few moments later, a door slammed shut.

Already regretting her outburst, Clara went in search of her. She had deposited the tray in the kitchen, then locked herself in her little bedroom. Clara knocked on the door tentatively. "Addie, dear? Are you all right?"

There was a long stretch of silence, but she heard the bedsprings squeak as Addie moved. "I'm doing what you asked and leaving you alone," she said at last.

Clara sighed. She knew she had been in the wrong, but she resented the guilt she was already feeling. "I'm sorry. I didn't mean to lash out at you like that."

More silence. She was about to walk away when Addie spoke again.

"Do you want me to leave?"

"No, of course not," Clara said, startled. She could hear drawers opening and closing and rapped on the door again. "Will you let me in?"

The lock clicked, and Addie let the door drift open, turning away as soon as Clara entered the room. Addie's suitcase was out on the bed, half-full with dresses tossed in willy-nilly.

"Come here," Clara said, her heart aching at the sight. She held out her arms, enveloping Addie in them. Addie trembled slightly, and Clara realized she was crying.

"I'm sorry," Addie said as tears leaked onto Clara's shoulder.

"I'm the one who's sorry," Clara said, holding her tight. "I shouldn't have snapped at you. I'd never want you to leave over something so silly."

Addie hugged her back, then tugged free and started putting her clothes away. "I'm not used to that, to be honest. Most of the time, one argument and it's over. You're very good to me."

Clara was outraged at how poorly Addie had been treated by the Hester Windermeres of her past. "I'm not like that. I've seen the effect it had on my father, to be shunned by his own father just for being himself. It's cruel."

"Well, what else can you expect from someone called Horrible Hank?" Addie said, rolling her eyes.

"How did you know that nickname?" Clara asked sharply.

For a split second, a look of stunned surprise flashed across Addie's face. She quickly hiked up a nervous smile. "You must have mentioned it sometime, maybe at a family dinner or something like that."

Clara shook her head. She couldn't forget Addie's initial expression when she'd realized she'd made a mistake. "No, I wouldn't have. We never use that around Mother and Father because it upsets them."

Addie shrugged in a forced-casual fashion. "Then maybe it was when we were with Fred and Albie, and your parents weren't there. In fact, I'm sure that's what happened."

Clara racked her brain, trying to remember a time when she and Addie had been alone with her brothers, and the topic of her grandfather had come up. As suspicious as Addie's reaction was, Clara still found herself hoping there was some rational explanation. She wanted to believe Addie, but she couldn't free herself of the certainty that things didn't add up.

"We stopped calling him that altogether after the will. It seemed rather shabby behavior to make fun of him after he left me everything, even if he was often unkind. In fact, the last time we ever used it was in…the telegram I got in France. You read it, didn't you?" Clara said, in a tone more accusatory than questioning.

Addie's face told her everything she needed to know, her mouth falling open and then rapidly closing. She dropped her eyes, refusing to meet Clara's gaze, and any hope Clara had that there was a legitimate explanation for Addie's behavior died. If Addie had seen the telegram by accident, she would have said so now. Clara couldn't think of any other reason Addie would keep it from her, not now when the stakes were so high.

Addie had come to Clara's cabin on the ship the very night she'd gotten the news about her inheritance. She had thought it a glorious coincidence, but now she saw it all in a different light. Sharp pain hit her chest like a knife between the ribs, even though she remained physically unscathed. She had spent months thinking Addie loved her for who she was, when it was nothing more than her grandfather's fortune she had been after.

"You…you knew about the money? I thought you…really cared for me, but all along, you *knew*." Clara's voice caught, and a few tears slipped out of her eyes.

"Clarabella, please listen—"

"*Don't*," Clara snarled, dashing the tears away. "Don't you dare call me that. And no more lies."

"All right." Addie held her hands up gingerly, as if she were trying to placate a frightened horse. "Yes, I knew. I found the telegram the night you got it. But that wasn't why I was drawn to you. I could talk to you. And you seemed so unsure of yourself, and I thought if I could just draw you out, boost your confidence…"

Clara let out an incredulous bark of laughter without an ounce of amusement. How could Addie possibly think that was a credible defense? "So I was some sad little mouse you thought you'd bless with your glorious attention? I was fine before you came along. I would've come back here and lived my life happily without you." She stared out unseeingly at the street below, not wanting Addie to see her face. Being the object of pity was somehow even worse than if Addie had been merely a gold digger. Every time Addie had sought her out, complimented her or laughed with her, it had all been pretend. Addie must have seen her as the most pathetic person alive. Humiliation burned in her chest at the thought, and she squeezed her fists so tight, her fingers hurt.

She remembered how much time Addie had spent with Hester Windermere before she'd set her sights on Clara. She doubted Addie had had the same level of pity for Miss Windermere, but Miss Windermere had probably figured out Addie's true purpose much quicker than Clara had. As soon as she'd lost out on one rich target, Addie had immediately moved on to the next. It was her good luck that Clara was so stupidly naive. Clara could barely stand to think about it. "I realize how bad it sounds," Addie said quietly to Clara's back. "And maybe it started out that way, but once I got to know you, to see you for all the amazing things you are, it changed. *I* changed. I didn't think I would ever feel like this for someone ever again, but then, you came along."

"I gave you every opportunity to be honest with me. After I found out about your family, I asked if there was anything else you hadn't told me. Why didn't you tell me then?"

Addie heaved a sigh. "I should have. That's obvious now. You were already so upset at finding out about my family, and I guess I thought it would be too much on top of that. I was afraid you would send me away or never trust me again."

Clara finally turned to face her. "How many others have there been?" she asked. She wasn't sure if she wanted an answer or not or if she'd even believe Addie's response.

"It's not like that," Addie said.

Clara was angrier than she even thought she could be. "Oh, really? What's it like, then? Because I have a feeling you've left a whole string of other women just like me in your wake."

Addie shook her head vehemently. "There's no one like you. Please understand. The way I feel about you…it's different from anyone else."

Clara couldn't help noticing Addie repeatedly sidestepping the question. She'd probably had this same argument with countless lovers. "How on earth can I trust you now after all the lies you've fed me?"

"If I could only find the words to explain how much I love you," Addie said, misery etched onto her features.

Clara stood still as stone. She desperately wanted to believe that Addie truly cared for her. Addie sounded sincere, and Clara could almost bring herself to accept her words. But Addie had sounded equally sincere when she'd told her the fake story of her family dying. How could Clara ever believe her?

"Please believe me," Addie whispered as if reading Clara's thoughts.

Which, Clara realized, she had been doing all along. Addie had always known just the right words to say to evoke her pity or guilt or gratitude. "Get out."

"Clara—" Addie started, sounding anguished.

Clara cut her off. "Just leave! I want you gone, do you hear me? I'll be back in an hour. If you're still here, I'm calling the police." She stormed out of the apartment and ran down the stairs. Waiting for the elevator might give Addie time to plead her case, and Clara didn't trust herself not to give in. By the time she reached the lobby, she was panting and had a stitch in her side.

She wandered the streets aimlessly, barely seeing the shops and offices as she strode past. Even with what she now knew, it was a struggle not to run back and stop Addie from leaving. She glanced at her watch and realized she had no idea how long it had been since she'd given Addie her one-hour ultimatum. She didn't have her purse but scrounged up enough change in her pocket to buy a cup of tea at a café. She splashed milk all over the saucer, her hand shaking as she tried to pour it in.

"Damn it," she exclaimed, slamming her trembling hands on the table. Heads turned to stare at her in alarm, and she flushed under their scrutiny.

Deciding it had been long enough, she abandoned her undrunk tea and made her way back home. As soon as she walked in, she realized it didn't feel like *home* anymore. She knew without a doubt that she had stayed away long enough, and Addie was gone. There was a strange echo when she snapped the door closed, as if Addie's absence had created a yawning chasm right there in the entryway.

Walking through each room in turn, she cataloged what Addie had left behind: the mink coat, all of her expensive new jewelry, even the books Clara had bought her. As far as Clara could tell, all she had taken away in her battered old suitcase was what she had already owned when they'd left France. In less than an hour, Addie had cleanly excised herself from what had only that morning been their happy home together.

Clara remembered Addie stealing her parents' money when she'd left their house on short notice and went into the living room. She pulled what appeared to be a copy of *The House of the Seven Gables* off the bookshelf. Years ago, Albie had painstakingly glued all of the pages together, then neatly cut out the middle to create a secret storage box. Until Pip, it had been Clara's favorite birthday present she had ever received. It currently held a hidden stash of several hundred dollars in case the apartment was ever burglarized, or she needed a lot of money at short notice. She counted the cash, surprised to find that every bit was fully present and accounted for. Addie had known about the hiding place and yet had left the money behind.

She must have forgotten it in her haste.

Clara thought of Pip and ran to check on him. Before this morning, it would never have occurred to her that Addie might take him away or do him any harm. Now that she understood that she had never known Addie at all, she realized anything was possible. She had only seen what she wanted to in Addie, not the real person underneath.

Pip was asleep in his cage with his head under his wing, but he woke when she opened the door. He chirped at her happily and fluttered onto her shoulder. She petted his soft head with the back of her fingers, relieved to find him safe and sound.

She gathered up every drawing she had ever done of Addie, tore them to shreds, then tossed the scraps into the fireplace. She hoped for some measure of relief or vindictive pleasure watching the bits of paper curl up and turn black as they fed the flames, but all she felt was a dull numbness.

The physical signs of Addie's presence might have been gone, but Clara couldn't erase the memories. Every time she walked in the door, they smacked her in the face. Whenever he was out of his cage, Pip flew from room to room, chirping hopefully. He always came back to settle on her shoulder, but she knew he had been looking for Addie. He started plucking out his own feathers, and the veterinarian she consulted cited stress or sadness as the likely cause.

She wouldn't admit it to anyone, but a part of her still hoped that she would wake up to find that it had all been a terrible misunderstanding, that Addie was coming back for good. Over the following weeks, she secluded herself in the apartment, ordering groceries by telephone. The only person she saw was Davis the doorman when he delivered them to her. She couldn't bear to speak to her parents, instead writing to them that she was ill and unable to come see them. Her mother telephoned to check on her after receiving the letter, and it was only by telling her that Addie was looking after her that Clara was able to stave off a visit.

The lie burned in her throat, but she couldn't bear the truth being known. Whenever she thought of how proud she'd been to have Addie on her arm or to hold her close as they danced, she cringed. How utterly foolish she had been to think that anyone would fall in love with her, that she had anything to recommend her except for half a million dollars. Everyone at Rosie's had probably known the score at first glance and were laughing at her behind her back for being so stupid and clueless. She could never go back there again.

CHAPTER TWENTY

As much as she tried not to think about Addie and what she might be doing, Clara kept wondering. She began visiting Julia multiple times a week, finding her cousin-in-law to be both pleasant company and a good source of information since she was still in occasional contact with Addie.

One Sunday in December, she asked Julia if she had heard from Addie. It was nearly Christmas, and Julia had tastefully decked out her sitting room. Little white candles sparkled all over the Christmas tree that was surrounded by wrapped presents for baby Henrietta.

"I had a letter from her the other day. She's now a live-in companion for someone named Rosie," Julia told her conspiratorially, bouncing Henrietta on her lap.

"Really?" A knife twisted in Clara's chest at how quickly Addie had moved on. Given what she'd learned about how duplicitous and mercenary Addie really was, it shouldn't have been a surprise, but it still shocked her how much it hurt.

Julia nodded. "I was so sorry to hear about the two of you parting on such bad terms. You always seemed so happy together."

"I thought we were," Clara said heavily. She hadn't told Julia the whole story, but Julia had such an ear for gossip that she had probably ferreted out enough details to put two and two together.

"Oh well. I'm sure you'll find another companion in no time," Julia said, patting her bracingly on the shoulder.

Harry came in then, so Clara quickly moved the conversation to safer topics. Thankfully, it wasn't difficult. Although the two of them still held each other at arm's length, fatherhood had changed Harry for the better. Julia watched him fondly as he enthused about Henrietta's latest accomplishment, the appearance of her first tooth. When Julia handed him a cloth to wipe Henrietta's mouth, he caught her hand and gave it a squeeze before releasing it. Clara was happy to see that their marriage had evolved into such a happy relationship, but the sight made her sad too. She missed the easy closeness she thought she had had with Addie.

Rosie's was already too tainted by memories for her to ever want to go back there, but Julia's news made her avoid the entire neighborhood. The last thing she wanted was to run into Addie, especially if she had to see her happily ensconced as Rosie's girl. Rosie wasn't as well off as Clara, but the bar no doubt did well enough for her to support Addie in modest comfort. She probably wouldn't be getting any more mink coats or diamond earrings, Clara thought savagely.

Julia didn't know the full nature of Addie and Clara's relationship, of course, but Clara considered her words seriously anyway. She asked around surreptitiously and found another underground bar like Rosie's, where she sat against the wall for a few nights before daring to ask a girl to dance. It was strange, holding someone else's hand and doing the same dance moves she'd done with Addie. The movements didn't flow as naturally, and she felt self-conscious in a way she never had with Addie. Her heart started racing, which she didn't think was solely attributable to the dancing. After the song ended, she pretended she had to go to the bathroom and fled.

When the lease on the apartment expired, Clara sold most of the furniture, packed up what little she planned to keep, and decamped to her parents' house with Pip. She couldn't bear staying in Boston, walking the same streets she had strode down with Addie so many times.

She wallowed under her mother's watchful eye and her father's blundering efforts to cheer her up until she could bear it no longer. Fred told her about a house for sale a mile or so away. The owner had lost his job in the Depression. He'd managed to find work in the western end of the state and was moving but hoped to return to Willoughby once the economy improved. His face lit up when she offered to rent his beloved home instead of buying it, and they quickly agreed on a fair price.

Her first night in the new house was unsettling, almost eerie. She realized she had never spent the night as the only person in a house, and every creak of the old place settling made her envision a robber breaking in. It didn't take her long to adjust, and soon, it was only thoughts of Addie that kept her awake.

She wondered what Addie was doing now. Had she gotten what she could out of Rosie and moved on, or did she have more genuine affection for Rosie than she'd had for Clara? She started running through every conversation she could remember having with Addie, searching for clues that she had missed in her obliviousness. That proved both painful and embarrassing, and she devoted her energies instead to charity work, reading, and anything else she could think of to distract herself.

Her pencils and paintbrushes sat unused, gathering dust. Every time she tried to draw, it felt wrong. The images she made were flat and joyless, like all the life had been sucked out of them. It depressed her too much, so she shut her supplies away in a spare bedroom and tried to forget she had ever loved art at all.

❖

Addie trudged up the stairs that led to Rosie's private quarters. She had been living there for over a month, and she still wasn't accustomed to having to tackle five flights of stairs every time she came or went. She missed Clara most of all, but the elevator in their old apartment building was a close second.

When she finally reached Rosie's apartment, she dropped her groceries on the kitchen table with a clunk and threw herself into a chair, kicking off her shoes with a groan. She knew she had better start fixing supper so Rosie could eat before going down to the bar, but she needed a minute to catch her breath and collect her thoughts.

She had seen Clara today as she'd left the butcher's. She'd ducked back into the shop until Clara passed, her heart pounding. Clara had either not seen her or done a very good job of pretending not to, for which Addie was grateful. She was shaken by the sight. Clara had looked wan and thin, as if she hadn't been eating properly. Her hair was back to its natural light brown shade and was getting long again. She'd scurried up the sidewalk, hunched over like she used to be when they had first met. She'd looked rather like the physical manifestation of how Addie felt.

Addie was doing a decent job of holding herself together externally, using powder to cover the bags under her eyes from not sleeping. Rosie was fond of her, but there were plenty of other beautiful women coming into the bar every night who'd jump at the chance of taking Addie's place. If she wanted to keep her position secure, she had to make sure she always looked and acted her best. It didn't matter that her heart had broken all over again watching Clara walk away or that guilt burned in her gut like an ulcer. She kept those feelings where they belonged, out of sight and as out of mind as she could manage.

"What's for supper?" Rosie stood in the kitchen doorway, running a hand through her short hair and blinking the sleep out of her eyes.

At first, Addie had adjusted her schedule to be nocturnal like Rosie, but spending night after night in the bar drained her both physically and emotionally. She kept hoping to see Clara, but an equal part of her dreaded it. Now that it had happened, she couldn't stop thinking about her. She had to force her attention back on Rosie.

"Tongue and lima beans," she said, and Rosie groaned. "I know they're not your favorites, but they were on sale. Everything's gotten so expensive these days. I also have the ingredients for an icebox cake. I'll bring down a piece later when it's done."

"It had better be two pieces to make up for the lima beans," Rosie grumbled.

"Hopefully, it'll be good enough to make you not regret having me here," Addie teased.

Rosie shook her head. "I don't regret that, even if it means tongue and lima beans every night."

"Aw, shucks," Addie said, and occupied herself with preparing the food while Rosie went to clean up and get dressed for work. Maybe if she kept herself busy enough, Addie could successfully avoid thinking about Clara until she forgot about her. That strategy hadn't worked so far, but who was to say it wouldn't eventually?

Unfortunately, it didn't even work all the way though supper. Rosie was gulping down her food, trying to finish the hated lima beans before she needed to be downstairs to open the bar. Addie had been keeping up a steady stream of commentary about whatever she could think of to keep the memory of Clara at bay, but her concentration slipped for a moment, and the words were out before she could stop them.

"I saw Clara today," she blurted. "She looked…well, she didn't look too happy. Have you seen her? Is she doing all right?"

Rosie set down her fork. "I hear things, but as far as I know, she hasn't been in since you broke up."

"What have you heard?"

"What does it matter? You're not together anymore, it's none of your business."

"Rosie," Addie said sternly.

Rosie groaned in protest but said, "Fine, fine. All I know is that she's been to Damien's place at least once. He saw her dancing with some broad. They left separately. Are you satisfied?"

"When was this?"

"A couple nights ago, I guess," Rosie said with a shrug. "What's the big deal? Are you still hung up on her or something? I always assumed it wasn't serious to you."

It stung that Rosie, who professed a certain amount of fondness for her, believed that she had merely been using Clara. Even Clara, the person Addie had thought knew her best in the world, thought so too.

❖

"You did love her, didn't you?" Rosie said a few days later.

Addie looked up from her magazine, startled but the sudden non sequitur. "Who?"

"Don't play dumb with me," Rosie said gently. "That act might work on other people, but I know you too well. You know who I'm talking about."

"Yes, I did. In fact, I…I still do."

"It's no good, is it? You and me?" Rosie said, looking at her intently.

Addie sighed. "No, I'm afraid it isn't. It's nothing you've done. You're really wonderful, you know. It's just…"

"It's just that I'm not Clara," Rosie finished for her.

"Right," Addie said sadly. She wished she did love Rosie the way that Rosie wanted her to. Perhaps in time, she would, but right now, Clara still filled her waking thoughts and haunted her dreams. It wasn't fair to expect Rosie to put up with that indefinitely.

"Maybe you can patch things up with her."

Addie laughed wryly. "I really don't think so. That bridge is well and truly burned."

"You never know," Rosie said with a shrug. "In my line of work, whenever you think you've seen everything, something totally unexpected always comes along."

"I don't deserve you, Rosie," Addie said, feeling a wave of tenderness and affection for her. "Or Clara, for that matter."

"Too right you don't, and don't you forget it," Rosie said, wagging her finger sternly and smirking.

Rosie let her sleep on the couch long enough for her to find a new living situation. It was time to forge her own path, to try relying on herself for a change. Maybe someday, she would find a place that felt like home, but she wasn't holding out hope. After all the pain she had caused Clara, she could no longer put herself in a position to hurt someone like that again.

It didn't take her long to find a position as a salesgirl in a bookshop and a room in a boarding house a few blocks away. She considered leaving Boston altogether to lessen the chances of running into Clara, but the thought of being so far away made her chest ache. Besides, she reasoned with herself, she was just as entitled to live here as anyone else. She certainly wasn't going back to Kansas, ever again if she could help it. This was her home now, and she was going to build the best life for herself that she possibly could.

Chapter Twenty-One

Boston, Massachusetts, 1930

It was barely worth getting the car out for the short trip to her parents' house, but Clara was pleased enough with her new Hudson that she'd decided to drive. Since moving back to Willoughby, she'd taken to spending two or three evenings a week with her family. It was the only time she felt truly comfortable.

Whenever she was out and about in town, people she barely knew would approach her and try to strike up conversation. The same classmates who'd mocked her in high school were eager to act like they were close friends who'd fallen out of touch. She'd indulged them the first few times it happened, but it inevitably turned into a would-be-casual mention of a lost job or a promising investment opportunity.

She made an exception for Gerald, the high school classmate she and Addie had seen at Rosie's. They met again at the Willoughby greengrocer's. Although at first, his eyes went wide with alarm, he'd seemed to calm down after Clara had pretended not to have seen him since graduation. He'd invited her to accompany him to a dance at the local veterans' hall, which she had been glad to do. She could use a friend here in town. Besides, he had always been kind to her, unlike most of the other boys, and he also had a penchant for art.

Their previous encounter had been too brief for her to notice that he had lost his right arm in the Great War. He was still able to dance well enough, but he'd described the slow and often frustrating process of learning to draw with his left hand.

"It's taken a long time, but I figured, why not? I don't have much else to do to fill the days," he'd said ruefully.

He'd received a small military pension for his injury, and since the stock market crash, it was his sole source of income. Jobs that he could work without his missing arm were few and far between in the best of times, he'd explained. Factory work was out of the question, and no shopkeeper wanted to hire a clerk who could only do half the work of someone else. Even if he'd had a college degree, he couldn't type or write well enough with his left hand for an office job. Clara wished she could share a bit of her own good fortune with him, but he wouldn't even let her buy him dinner.

"I'd much rather earn my living than be a charity case," he'd said firmly, and she'd had no choice but to acquiesce.

Gerald's predicament continued to bother her, and she brought it up over dinner with her brothers.

"It's a real shame," Albie said, stroking his chin thoughtfully. "I know a lot of fellows in similar situations. In some ways, it's almost worse for the ones with shell shock. They struggle just as much as someone like Gerald, but because they don't have any physical scars, people don't understand why they can't go back to their normal lives."

"Someone should do something about it," Clara declared. "Help them get job training and placements and so on."

"If only we knew someone with a large amount of money and a lot of free time on their hands," Fred said.

Clara rolled her eyes at him. "I've picked up on your subtle clue. I'll need help, though. Lots of it. Both of you and probably Gerald too."

Albie groaned. "We're being drafted again."

"As if you're doing something more important with your time," Clara scoffed.

When Clara brough it up with Gerald later, he was enthusiastic about the idea and quickly agreed to join in their efforts. Clara was daunted by the amount of need all around them, but she had spent so much of the past six months moping about over Addie that it felt good to have something constructive to focus on.

She wondered if Addie was still with Rosie, and how they were weathering the Depression. So many people had lost everything, even the very wealthy, that probably a lot of the women Addie normally would have targeted were now as broke as she was. Clara knew it was only luck that she herself hadn't lost much. She hoped Addie wasn't having too tough a time. Then she reminded herself that she didn't care, and she almost believed it.

❖

"I'm truly sorry, Miss Barnes, but there simply aren't enough customers for me to justify keeping this many staff. Since you're the newest, I'm afraid I'll have to let you go."

Addie nodded stoically. Mr. Greves sounded genuinely regretful, and she couldn't deny the truth in his words. In the two months she had been working at the perfume counter in his department store, she was lucky to have made three or four sales a day, and more than once, she'd sold nothing at all. The longer the Depression went on, the more people were cutting back on luxuries. Perfume was hardly a necessity if they were having trouble keeping their children fed.

The thought didn't make it any easier for Addie as she packed up her locker for the last time. She'd made a small hourly wage in addition to commissions, but it had been barely enough to cover her rent at Mrs. Hamilton's boarding house. She was paid up through the end of the week, but Mrs. Hamilton was hardly the charitable type to let her stay any longer without payment. Come Monday morning, she'd have nowhere to go.

She headed for the employment agency on Bristol Street, but the line of other job seekers snaked all the way out of the building and around the corner. Before she could decide whether it was worth it to join the waiting crowd, a harassed-looking man pushed through the throng around the door to announce that the agency was closed for the day, and they'd all have to come back tomorrow. The crowd grumbled angrily but soon dispersed.

She returned to the boarding house, bypassing the dining room. Dinner was an extra fifty cents a day, and she could no longer afford the splurge. Upstairs, she looked around the little room that probably wouldn't be hers for much longer. It wasn't much, but it was clean and safe and felt like the closest thing to a home she'd had since leaving Clara's. She had been living there for four months, long enough that she had hung the frame containing Clara's drawing of her in the lavender field.

Sometimes the sight of it made shame and regret burn in her throat, and she went days without looking at it. Other times, it seemed to draw her gaze magnetically. It took her back to that brief period when things had seemed much simpler, although she probably hadn't felt that way at the time.

She got up earlier each morning than the day before, but she never managed to get to the employment agency in time to have any chance at getting a work placement. Men with families to support were given priority, and there were far too many of them also looking for work.

She tried going from shop to shop but met with no luck. As soon as the shopkeepers realized she wasn't there to buy anything, they shooed her away. She tried restaurants, factories, commercial laundries, and every other type of business she could think of. Her typing skills were minimal, and she didn't know shorthand at all, so she didn't bother with any offices. Those that weren't already fully staffed wouldn't even give her the time of day without the requisite skills.

She held out hope that surely something would come along in the nick of time like it always did, but her desperation grew as the calendar crept closer to Monday. By Saturday, she was approaching full-fledged panic. She changed tactics and went through her entire address book, trying to think of anyone she'd ever met in Boston who might be able to give her work or lend her a little money to tide her over.

Rosie and the rest of her crowd were eager to help, but many of them were in as desperate need as she was or even worse off. The bar had been raided a few months ago. Thankfully, they had only been slapped with a liquor charge, not public indecency, but it had scared away much of the clientele. The bar had never regained its previous level of business. Even Rosie was struggling to keep a roof over her head, and practically every square foot of floor space in her living area was someone else's designated sleeping spot already. She gave Addie a glass of bathtub gin and a few dollars, but aside from a sympathetic hug, that was all she had to offer. Addie accepted it all with gratitude and a promise to pay back the money as soon as she could.

After that, she was well and truly running out of options. Another problem was that she'd met most of her acquaintances with Clara. Even if Clara hadn't told them of her duplicity and warned them against her, it didn't feel right to turn to Clara's friends and family for help.

By the time Mrs. Hamilton apologetically but firmly turned her out on Monday morning, she was feeling a good deal less scrupulous. She hadn't eaten in over twenty-four hours, and anyone who could possibly help her was fair game.

Julia, Harry, and baby Henrietta were out of the country, their housekeeper informed her. Addie wasn't sure how much they would have done for her if they'd been there, since their loyalty was to Clara, after all. Still, it was dismaying not to have the chance to find out. At the very least, she knew Julia would not have sent her away without feeding her first.

At last, she was down to her very last option. She went back to the apartment building where she and Clara had lived together.

"Hello, Miss Barnes," Davis the doorman said, tipping his cap to her.

"Is Miss Cooper in, please?" Addie asked. Officially, he wasn't supposed to tell her, but he had always liked her and might make an exception.

"You haven't heard?" he asked, his eyebrows rising in surprise.

Cold dread gripped Addie's heart. "Heard what? What's happened to her?" *Please, God, let her be all right.*

"She moved out as soon as her lease was up. It was a real shame, losing first you and then her. You girls brightened the building up considerably. Now it's just the old geezers left, myself included," he said with a chuckle.

Clara hadn't left a forwarding address, but he thought she had gone back to her hometown. Addie thanked him and left, relieved that Clara was unharmed but crestfallen not to find her. She considered asking Davis for a small loan, but she still had enough pride left not to want her former doorman to know how far she had fallen.

CHAPTER TWENTY-TWO

Addie hid in the bathroom for the forty-minute train ride to Willoughby, narrowly avoiding the conductor collecting the eighty-cent fare she could ill afford to spend. She couldn't remember the name of the street Clara's family lived on, so she consulted the local directory in the train station phone booth.

She was taken aback to see that above the listing for "Cooper, Mr. and Mrs. Daniel" was one for "Cooper, C." She had assumed Clara would go back to living with her family, but she might have been living on her own instead. She wrote down both addresses, checking the little town map at the front of the book to make sure she could find them.

They were both to the west of the town center, so she started walking down the busy main street while she considered which house to try first. Even if Clara wasn't living with her parents, they would surely know where she was. But would they tell her? She had no idea how much Clara had told her family about their falling out, and they might not be willing to speak to her. Perhaps she should check on the solo C. Cooper first.

Geography made the choice for her, as C. Cooper's street was closer to town. The houses she passed all looked like classic Americana, neat little Cape Cods of varying colors with well-kept lawns. Most had an automobile in the driveway, and she sensed that most of the residents hadn't been hit too hard by the Depression. Clara had loved the Boston apartment fiercely, and it was hard to picture her living here with her flapper style and artistic nature.

She reached the house that might have been Clara's and looked for anything that might tell her whether or not she was on the right track. It was a two-story Cape with gabled windows like the rest of the neighboring houses, painted tan with sage green shutters. A shiny new Hudson Greater Eight sat in the driveway, the red and blue luxury car standing out from the fleet of more affordable Model As and Chryslers owned by the rest of the neighborhood. She took that as a promising sign since it was unlikely anyone else here had the resources to buy such a nice vehicle.

That was as good a reason as any to take the chance and approach. She had run out of pride days ago, but now her nerve was teetering too. She steeled herself and walked up the brick-lined path to the front door.

She took a deep breath and knocked, praying to whatever deity there might be that Clara would take pity on her. After a minute or so, the door swung open. Clara was framed in the doorway, looking just as beautiful as Addie remembered.

"What do *you* want?" Clara snapped without preamble.

Addie supposed she ought to have planned out what she was going to say, but it probably wouldn't have done any good anyway. As soon as she saw Clara, her mind went blank. She wanted to hurl herself into Clara's arms like no time had passed, to beg forgiveness and then slip back into their life together.

"May I come in?" she asked.

"Absolutely not. Say what you're here for, and then, go away."

That response wasn't exactly promising, but Addie was here because she had no other options. She forged ahead. "I lost my job and my living situation. I was hoping you might be able to help me out."

Clara's face twisted into a mirthless smile. The expression didn't suit her, and Addie felt an involuntary shudder at the coldness in it. "And why," she said slowly, dragging the words out, "why on God's green earth would I do anything to help *you*?"

"I know you have every reason to hate me. And no reason to trust me. Believe me, I wouldn't be here if I had any other choice. I don't want any money, I'll work for free, whatever needs doing. I just need something to eat and somewhere safe to sleep."

Clara snorted derisively. "There's only one thing I know you're good at, and you certainly don't give that away for free."

Addie winced. She deserved that, she supposed, but the words seemed even harsher coming from Clara. The Clara she knew would never have treated someone this way. This person was a stranger. She had no rejoinder, so she kept quiet.

Clara crossed her arms and glared at her. Each second felt like a lifetime as Addie waited to see what she would say. Her face, once so open, stayed closed as a series of unreadable expressions flickered across it. Without warning, she slammed the door in Addie's face.

Addie blinked at the abruptness of the dismissal. Well, that was that. Her last hope was gone. She wondered dully if the local church might let her sleep in a pew for a night or two. She might as well try. It was right next to the train station, after all. She couldn't afford a ticket back to Kansas, but maybe she could hide in a freight car. If she threw herself on her parents' mercy, they might let her come back. The very idea filled her with dread, but she couldn't see that she had any other choice.

She picked up her suitcase and trudged back toward the sidewalk. She felt every step of the two mile walk into the center of Willoughby, and by the time she reached the church, she was limping from a blister on her left heel. The heat had only intensified; she could feel sweat dripping down her face, and her blouse was plastered to her back.

Her bad luck continued; every door of the church was locked up tight, and her knocking received no response. *So much for Christian charity.* She wanted to scream in frustration. True, she was no angel, but she had done nothing to deserve this.

She sat on the church steps until a policeman on his rounds shooed her away, looking at her suspiciously. She could feel his watchful eyes on her back and didn't dare go to the train yard just yet. Instead, she took a seat at the counter in the little café next to the station, sliding her suitcase under her feet.

A nickel got her a mediocre cup of coffee and an abandoned copy of that day's *Willoughby Morning Herald*, snatched up from an empty table before the harried-looking waitress could clear it away. Her stomach growled at the scent of bacon wafting out from the kitchen, but her money was dwindling quickly. She added extra sugar to her coffee instead, hoping it would give her the energy she needed.

She flipped through the newspaper until she found the train schedule. The commuter trains were no good to her; she had gotten lucky on the way here, but the conductors were far too used to keeping a close eye on who was onboard and would be sure to notice that she didn't have a ticket. Her suitcase would make her even more conspicuous among the crowd of businessmen.

Instead, she looked at the freight routes that passed through Willoughby. The town was small enough that only a handful stopped there each day, and the next westbound freight train wouldn't arrive until nearly midnight. It wasn't even suppertime yet, so she was in for a long wait.

She lingered in the café, the waitress—Arlene, according to her name tag—glaring at her sourly every time she came by to refill Addie's coffee until she gave in to her hunger and sacrificed a precious quarter for a toasted cheese sandwich. She took tiny bites, trying to make it last, but when she was done, she felt somehow even hungrier than before. At eight o'clock, the restaurant closed, and Arlene chivvied her out the door, locking it behind her emphatically.

Main Street was already almost deserted, most of the shops locked and lights extinguished. Even the waiting area of the train station was closed, the last passenger train of the day having departed over an hour ago. She walked past it toward the freight depot, feeling conspicuous.

The gate to the depot was chained shut, but she thought she'd be able to climb over it if she couldn't find another way in. She rattled the bars of the gate to test them.

"Who's there?"

The beam of a flashlight cut through the darkness just beyond the gate, most likely a night watchman on patrol. She hurried past the depot before he could spot her. She would have to be stealthy to avoid detection.

She found the dark doorway of a closed shop that was set back enough from the sidewalk to shield her in darkness. That would have to do for a waiting place.

She heard a car approaching and tried to duck farther into the shadows, but the driver had seen her. She flinched when it slowed and honked at her, ice coursing through her veins. She gripped her suitcase tightly, deciding she could use it as a bludgeon to defend herself if necessary. As the driver rolled down the window, she wondered if she ought to go on the offensive and attack them before they could attack her.

But she recognized the distinctive red and blue vehicle and loosened her grip on the suitcase with relief.

"You can sleep in the room above the garage." Clara's expressionless voice emerged from the darkness of the car. "Hop in."

"Thank you, thank you so much. You've no idea...thank you," Addie sputtered, clambering into the car as quickly as she could. Her heart still raced from her moments of fear.

Clara ignored her for the entire ten minute drive. She'd left the house without her gloves, and she grasped the steering wheel so tightly that her knuckles shone white. Addie wanted to ask what had caused Clara to change her mind, but she feared doing anything that might make her change it again.

When they pulled into Clara's garage, she turned toward Addie and eyed her sternly. "I want a five dollar deposit for utilities and damages."

It would wipe out most of her little safety net, but the amount was more than fair. Addie dug around in her wallet, eventually producing a two-dollar bill, a crumpled one-dollar bill, and an assortment of change to make up the rest.

Clara accepted the money wordlessly, counting out the coins carefully, then handed her a key on a little loop of twine. "If you want to cook, you'll have to figure something out for yourself because you're not setting foot in my house. The less I see of you, the better."

"I really can't tell you how much I appreciate this," Addie said fervently. "You won't regret it."

"I already do," Clara muttered. She went inside the house without another word and slammed the door again, but Addie thought it was with slightly less force than before.

Addie walked around the outside of the garage and climbed the rickety wooden stairs at the back. The key Clara had given her stuck in the lock a bit, but with some jiggling, she was able to get the door open.

A wave of hot humid air hit her; the room was stifling and probably hadn't been aired out in months. It couldn't have been more than ten feet by ten, the gabled roof of the garage reducing the usable space farther. A rusty metal cot sat along one wall, a rolled-up mattress on it. There were no pillows or bedding and no other furniture.

She set her suitcase inside the door and tested the taps of the wash basin along the far wall. Both hot and cold produced the same tepid water, but she wet her handkerchief to dab at her face and neck with it gratefully before gulping down several handfuls. A door next to the wash basin revealed a tiny room with a pull-chain toilet.

She locked the door, kicked off her shoes, and opened the room's two little windows to try to tempt the faint breeze into the oven of the room to little avail. She rolled out the mattress onto the cot. Based on the musty smell, she thought it likely predated President Cleveland's first term, but she was in no position to complain. She wadded up her raincoat to use as a pillow, draped her damp handkerchief over her forehead, and was asleep almost instantly.

❖

"How could you be so stupid," Clara chastised herself as she fruitlessly tried to punch her pillow into a more comfortable shape.

She could sense Addie on the property, even though she was out in the garage, far away. Addie was cunning and manipulative, had done nothing but lie and take advantage of her, so why had Clara broken her promise to herself and stepped in to help her? She should have left Addie to her fate; whatever that was, it would have been no worse than she deserved.

Maybe she was being unfair. She couldn't imagine the desperation that must have led Addie to her door. Her family wasn't well off, and she'd faced a perilously uncertain future before her inheritance, but even in her worst times, she had never been on the brink of homelessness. Flawed though Matilda and Harry might be, they'd have never left her to starve.

Clara had slammed the door in Addie's face, afraid her soft heart would give in. But even without Addie in front of her, the image of her on Clara's doorstep, her clothes threadbare and her cheeks wan and sunken with hunger, had haunted her. Despite it all, Clara had loved her once, or at least, the person she had pretended to be. Addie no doubt thought her hopelessly naive, and maybe she was. Perhaps she should try to be more like Addie, look out only for herself, but that wasn't who she was.

Addie had taken enough from her—money, trust, dignity—she didn't get to take her values too. Clara wouldn't leave Addie to fend for herself on the street, and if that made her pathetic, so be it. She would have to be on her guard, take care that she didn't fall for Addie's act again.

Pip cheeped from his perch next to her bed. He had been in his cage when Addie had come calling, thank heaven for small favors. He had a remarkably long memory for people, and she had no doubt that if he'd heard Addie's voice, he would have come fluttering out to greet her.

She sat up in bed and held her hand out. He hopped onto it and swayed to keep his balance as she brought him to her shoulder. The bald patches where he had plucked out his feathers had grown in, and he was as beautiful and healthy-looking as the day Addie had bought him. She hoped this new arrangement wouldn't unsettle him all over again. It was certainly unsettling enough to her.

CHAPTER TWENTY-THREE

Addie awoke in the middle of the night drenched in sweat and utterly confused about where she was. It came back to her in bits and pieces. Clara had saved her yet again, little though she deserved it. She had to find some way to make it up to Clara if she could. Now that she had a roof over her head, she could focus on that. At the very least, she could try to pay back some of the money Clara had spent on her.

The next morning, she walked back into town to try to find a job. The results weren't any more promising than her experience in Boston, and by suppertime, she had nothing to show for it but sore feet and a growling stomach. She had no way to cook in her little garret room, and she was too hungry to care that she was almost broke.

She went back to the café by the train station where she'd lingered the night before and spent the last quarter of the money Rosie had lent her on a sandwich. If she wasn't able to find work, she would have to hope that Willoughby had a decently stocked soup kitchen where she could at least get something to eat every day.

The café was bustling, and the same waitress from last night, Arlene, was being run ragged. She appeared to be the only person working there, aside from the cook. Plates of food piled up in the serving window before Arlene could get to them, and Addie could hear some of the other diners grumbling complaints to each other. The cook emerged as Arlene finally made it back behind the counter.

"What's the holdup?" he hissed, jerking his head in the direction of the waiting plates of food.

"*You* try serving an entire restaurant full of people all by yourself.

I won't put up with this any longer, I mean it," Arlene snapped. "You need more help around here."

Addie's ears perked up at the outburst. She sensed an opportunity. "Excuse me," she said sweetly. Both Arlene and the cook turned to look at her with similarly forbidding expressions. She forged ahead anyway. "I couldn't help but overhear. Are you in need of another waitress?"

"Do you have any experience waiting tables?" the man barked.

She nodded. Since part of her duties on the riverboat had included being in the dining room at mealtimes, she didn't think it too much of a stretch to say she had relevant work history. Besides, she was a fast learner and had the added incentive of being desperate for any kind of legitimate employment.

"Twenty cents an hour, plus one meal every shift. Take it or leave it," he grunted, grabbing two plates from the window and shoving them into Arlene's hands.

The wages were almost insultingly low, but she wasn't in much of a position to refuse. Her living expenses were minimal, thanks to Clara's generosity, so she would simply have to make do. At least she knew she would have one meal a day. She was lucky to find work at all in a town as small as Willoughby. However long it might take, this was the start of making her amends to Clara.

CHAPTER TWENTY-FOUR

Clara prodded pointlessly at the tomato plant in her back garden with her trowel, willing it to do anything other than sit there listlessly. It obeyed in a monkey's paw sort of way; she would have sworn it withered even further before her very eyes.

She sighed heavily. She had had grand dreams of a backyard bursting with vegetable plants, enough to lessen her own grocery bill and possibly even donate to the church if there were some left over. Alas, it seemed it wasn't to be.

"You're watering them too much," Addie said softly from behind her.

Clara saw her shadow move across the plant as she walked tentatively closer. She forced herself not to turn to look, staring fixedly at the plant. She wondered if she'd ever reach the point when she didn't instinctively want to turn toward Addie like a sunflower hoping the sun would condescend to send a few rays in its direction.

Addie knelt beside her. There was still at least two feet of space between them, but it was the closest they had been since Clara had brought her here in the car. She fought the urge to move, although whether it was to be nearer or to run away, she couldn't have said.

"You're watering them too much," Addie repeated. She took the trowel from Clara's hand and dug at the soil around the roots of the plant.

Clara recoiled as a cloud of little insects flew up. "Ew."

Addie smiled. "Ew, indeed. Those are fungus gnats. They're feeding on fungus growing in the soil because it hasn't had a chance to dry out between waterings. With this soil, the way that it retains water…I'd say you only need to water them once a week or so. Less if it's been rainy."

"Oh dear," Clara said. She had been watering them daily, afraid they'd shrivel and die. "No wonder they haven't produced any tomatoes."

"If I may?" Addie sounded hesitant, but Clara reminded herself that Addie was more than capable of making her voice sound any way she wished.

"What?" Clara snapped. It came out more harshly than she intended, but better to offend Addie than to give her a toehold to force her way into Clara's heart again.

Addie flinched so minutely that Clara probably wouldn't have noticed if she hadn't been watching. "I know you'd rather not see me around, but if you're willing…well, I grew up on a farm, and I know quite a lot about gardening and things. I could help you."

Clara folded her arms protectively. "I suppose that would be all right."

Addie gave her a tentative smile and turned back to the tomato plant, digging in with the trowel to scrape away the fly-infested soil. Clara stood and watched her for a moment, torn between her natural urge to help and her resolve not to give Addie any leeway. She settled for a compromise, unhooking the garden shed key from her key ring and handing it to Addie without looking at her.

"Make sure to lock it up when you're not out here. The people next door had their tools stolen a few weeks ago. You can use whatever's in there, but if you need to buy more supplies, that's on your dime."

"I'll get started right away," Addie said eagerly, tucking the key in her pocket.

"Fine," Clara said, marching away without another word.

In the weeks that followed, Addie threw herself into bringing the garden to its full potential. Whenever she wasn't working at the café, she was weeding, pruning, or digging new vegetable beds. It brought back mostly unwelcome memories from her childhood, but a few pleasant ones filtered in. She recalled how she used to toddle around the porch, shelling peas for her grandmother when she was too small to do anything else. She nurtured the garden as she wished she had done with her relationship with Clara.

She became a regular at the little hardware store in downtown Willoughby, befriending the owner and his family. His wife gifted her a handwoven straw hat, a welcome shield during the hours she spent in the sun. His daughter gave her rides home in the store pickup truck if she was making a delivery close to Clara's house, frequently casting admiring glances in Addie's direction.

The girl was breezy and outgoing, funny and easy to talk to. Addie wished she reciprocated her interest and could embark on a fun, low stakes summer romance, but something held her back. It was probably just staying in Clara's garage that was making her reluctant. Clara had been kind enough to give her a place to live when she had nowhere else to go, and it would have been poor thanks indeed to flaunt a new relationship in her face.

As June turned into July and the weather heated up, the long afternoons coincided with more to do in the garden than ever. One particularly brutal Sunday, Clara emerged from the house with a glass of iced lemonade. She was still in the tailored green skirt suit she always wore to church, her hair curled and pinned neatly under her hat. Addie's heart ached at how pretty she looked.

Clara didn't quite look at Addie as she placed the glass on the patio table with a soft *thunk*. "You've been working hard. It wouldn't do for you to get heatstroke with this sun."

"Thank you," Addie said, touched by the gesture. A pettier person might have enjoyed seeing the woman who'd hurt her laboring away day after day, but she couldn't believe that of Clara. She took a sip of the lemonade, the cool sweetness welcome on her parched throat.

Clara opened her mouth as if to speak, then closed it again. "You're welcome," she said at last. She looked as if she wanted to say more.

Addie wished she would. This small overture of kindness made her long for the connection they had once shared. She didn't know if she ought to risk trying to prolong the conversation, but she'd never gotten anywhere by being timid. "How has your art been going?"

It was the wrong question to ask. Clara's face shuttered, and she pursed her lips unhappily. "I haven't been doing much lately. I can't seem to find inspiration anywhere. I don't think I've made anything really good since…well, in the last two years."

"Oh. I'm very sorry to hear that." Apparently, art was yet another thing she had ruined for Clara.

Clara shrugged. "I've done some landscapes and still lifes and the like, but nothing really inspired. Nothing like the drawing I did of you in the lavender field."

Addie swallowed hard. She was surprised Clara had mentioned it. "This is quite the heatwave we're having, isn't it?"

Nice going, Addie, talking about the weather. How boring can you possibly be?

"Yes," Clara said. "We're going to the White Mountains but not until the end of the summer. Fred couldn't take time off work until then. It's a pity because it's much cooler there now."

"He's still working?" Addie was surprised. Clara's fortune should have been plenty to support her entire family, but maybe the Depression had hit her harder than Addie had realized.

Clara stiffened. "He chooses to. He happens to find meaning in hard work. I take care of my family, thank you very much," she said coldly. "He and Albie started a charity to help veterans learn new skills to find employment. It's extremely busy right now, as I'm sure you can imagine."

"That's certainly a noble cause. I didn't mean to offend you," Addie said. She couldn't seem to stop putting her foot in her mouth. "Anyway, I'd better get back to work."

It was better to end the conversation than to keep upsetting Clara, but Addie was still sad to see her walk away without another word.

Clara's book discussion group rotated among the members' homes, and this week it was Clara's turn to host. Usually, Addie steered clear of Clara's infrequent guests. She hadn't recognized any of them other than Clara's family, and she remembered that Clara hadn't had a lot of close friends in Willoughby. Most likely, Clara hadn't told any of her casual acquaintances the scandalous story of her relationship with Addie or the aftermath. The rest of the book group probably thought Addie was just hired help. Still, she was reluctant to have anyone see her face shiny with sweat or her dirt-stained clothes, even if they were strangers.

With the temperature still stifling, the group met outside on the patio. Addie made herself scarce, hiding out in the oven of her little garret. Although she couldn't make out individual words, the sound of voices floated up to her room. Finally, she heard the group disperse, waited a few minutes to make sure the coast was clear, then went downstairs. She wanted to do a little more in the garden before the mosquitos came out in force at dusk.

She pulled up short when she rounded the corner of the garage and saw that Clara was still sitting out on the patio with one of the book group members, a pretty blond woman whose name Addie didn't know. The woman giggled as Clara talked, her hand resting on Clara's forearm. Addie froze at the sight. She would have thought that Clara would hate being the center of attention, but evidently, she'd lost the shyness that had struck Addie so powerfully when they'd first met. When had that happened? Even when they'd been living together in Boston, she had tended to rely on Addie to expand their social circle.

What had she thought, that Clara would sit at home alone, pining over her forever? In all honesty, it had never occurred to her that Clara might someday move on with another lover, might indeed have already done so. But Clara was beautiful, kind, funny, and, of course, rich. Of course someone else was bound to notice at some point. It caused something deep in Addie's chest to curdle, a mixture of jealousy, regret, and disgust with her own self-centeredness.

Clara and the woman were so wrapped up in their conversation that Addie was able to slink away unseen. Even when Clara had been angry with her, she at least *noticed* that Addie was there. This was like being invisible, and Addie didn't like it one bit.

CHAPTER TWENTY-FIVE

Rebecca Davies hung back so long after the book discussion ended that Clara wondered if she was fishing for a dinner invitation. It wasn't until hours after Rebecca had finally left that it occurred to Clara that Rebecca had been flirting with her. She knew it didn't mean anything—it was widely known around town that the happily married Rebecca flirted with anyone who stood still long enough but would never dream of cheating on her husband—but it was still flattering. She was a little embarrassed not to have noticed, though. A tiny, mean-spirited part of her wished Addie had seen.

See, you're not the only one who's ever taken an interest in me.

Addie hadn't been around all day, though. She never was when Clara had guests over to the house. Clara didn't see her until the following morning.

"Do you think…could I possibly see Pip sometime? I miss him," Addie asked hesitantly as Clara brought her lemonade.

It wasn't that unreasonable a request, Clara supposed. However much she might like to think of Addie as an irredeemable monster, she and Pip did have a special bond. "I'll bring his cage out to the patio."

Addie beamed, and Clara had to turn away so she wouldn't stare. It was unfair how distractingly beautiful she was.

Clara tried not to feel jealous as Pip started chirping in excitement and jumping up and down with delight the moment he saw Addie. She had eyes only for Pip, cooing at him lovingly through the bars of his cage.

"I've missed you too, Sir Pippins," she told him.

He hopped on his perch a few times, then fluttered toward the door of the cage. When it didn't open, he pecked at it, then screeched angrily.

Addie clucked her tongue at him disapprovingly. "Now, Pip, you know you can't fly loose outside. You might get hurt or lost." She raised her hand to the bars.

"Don't—" Clara started to say, but Addie had already put a finger through before she could finish the warning.

"Ouch!" Addie cried, examining her now bleeding finger. In his overwhelmed excitement, Pip had pecked her. "I knew he might do that, but it seemed worth the risk."

"Do you need a bandage?"

Addie held out her hand so Clara could see. "I don't think it's too bad. As long as the bleeding stops soon, it should be fine."

Without thinking, Clara raised Addie's hand and took her injured finger into her mouth, sucking on it gently. The iron tang of Addie's blood hit her tongue as she ran it over the wound.

Addie stared at her with wide eyes, her chest rising and falling rapidly. "I…"

Sanity hit, and Clara shoved Addie's hand away. "I'm sorry, I don't know why I did that. I need to, um, go do…something."

She could hear Addie calling her name as she ran away but didn't slow down until she was inside the house. Why on earth had she done that? She must have been crazy.

Even so, over the next few days, she couldn't shake the feeling of Addie's finger in her mouth or the memories it evoked. It was mostly lurid ones at first, of long sleepless nights in each other's arms, but those soon gave way to more tender moments. Addie knitting matching scarves for Clara, Pip, and herself. The untold hours of Clara painting or drawing in the park while Addie kept her company. Addie going out for cinnamon rolls from the bakery just because she knew Clara hadn't slept well, and they were her favorite.

Stop it. Addie had humiliated her, played her for a fool. She couldn't simply pretend that had never happened. But nor could she believe it had all been an act, despite what she knew now about Addie's motivations.

❖

Clara couldn't seem to stop herself from focusing on Addie when she was at home, so she seized any excuse she could find to stay out and about. The charity she had started with her brothers and Gerald proved the perfect opportunity.

It wasn't merely an excuse. There was genuinely a great need for their services, and she felt like they were merely scratching the surface no matter how much they did. Albie and Fred were organizing a program to train veterans to work in funeral homes, one of the few industries still thriving. Even with the Depression lingering, people still needed to bury their loved ones.

Clara made visits to try to convince local farmers to hire some of their veteran clients as workers and donate any unsold produce to their soup kitchen. She tried her best, but she didn't have Addie's easy manner and effortless charm. They had certainly worked on Clara, and she imagined it would be just as effective with the farmers. She toyed with the idea of bringing Addie along and seeing if they had better luck as a team, but that would have meant hours in the car together multiple times a week. She didn't trust herself to spend that much time alone in close proximity to Addie and not fall for her again.

After lackluster results on her first few attempts, she invited Gerald to accompany her. Not only was he a big help with the farmers, but the long car trips between destinations also gave them their first real chance to talk openly without fear of eavesdroppers. She wound up telling him everything about her history with Addie, from their first meeting to Addie moving into her garage. She felt physically lighter afterward, having finally shared the full story with another person.

Gerald gave a low whistle as she finished. "You're good people, Clara. Not a lot of other people would let her stay after what she did to you. It sounds like she's cleaned up her act a bit, though."

"Yes," she said, thinking it over. "I really do think she's changed. She's out in that garden every day, even though she never even liked doing that work on the farm. I've been able to contribute a lot to the soup kitchen because of her."

"She started things with you before she knew about the money, right? Maybe her feelings were genuine."

"But she lied to me for months," she protested.

He held up his hands placatingly. "I know, and you'd every right to throw her out like you did. All I know is that it's hard enough when you're like us to find someone in the first place, let alone to be able to be together. I'd give anything to be able to live with the person I love, even if he knew I was rich. I can tell you love her from the way you talk about her. Otherwise, you wouldn't care so much this long after you broke up."

She considered his words long after they parted ways that afternoon. She couldn't deny the truth in them. Instead of the bitter sting she had expected she'd always feel when she thought about Addie, her spirits were lifted every time she looked outside and saw her in the garden. Even when Addie wasn't there, the signs of her presence were everywhere: the flourishing garden, the refrigerator full of vegetables, her blouses wafting in the breeze on the clothesline. She tried to look for the best in everyone, but she might have taken it too far and put Addie on a bit of a pedestal before. She knew her more now, the flaws that Addie tried to keep hidden. It wasn't like she herself was perfect either. Maybe she should consider giving Addie another chance.

CHAPTER TWENTY-SIX

S o you're still here," Matilda Cooper said, managing to inject a surprising amount of venom into just four words.

Addie had been weeding in the garden when Matilda arrived unexpectedly, and with pleading eyes, Clara had asked her to join them for coffee on the patio. Although she couldn't think of much she would less rather do, she couldn't let Clara down when she needed her. She was regretting it now, though, as she bore the brunt of Matilda's beady-eyed glare.

Clara jumped in while Addie was still trying to formulate a response. "Yes she is, and she's my guest, so I'll thank you to treat her with respect."

Guest was perhaps an overly generous description of Addie's living situation at the moment, but she was too busy internally cheering Clara on to care about semantics.

Matilda's mouth fell open, and she visibly bristled. "Sheer impertinence, all of you young girls. You've become nearly as bad as Julia." Her face darkened further at the mention of her daughter-in-law.

Although Matilda didn't mean it as a compliment, Addie thought it was quite flattering. Matilda had never forgiven Julia for stealing her beloved son away, but Addie liked her very much.

"Thank you," Clara said sweetly, clearly thinking along the same lines as Addie.

"Your grandfather did you no favors. All of that money can't buy you manners or class. It's no wonder, given how you grew up, but what a waste."

"All right, that's it." Addie hurled her napkin onto the table, causing her coffee cup to rattle ominously in its saucer. "I'm sick of your barbs about Clara and her family. You want to talk about class? She's got more in her little finger than you could ever dream of. And manners? You might know which fork to use at a fancy dinner or the proper way to address the duke of such-and-such, but you're horrid. Clara's put up with your nonsense for years, not just because she needed to but because she's kind and good and generous. Well, I'm none of those things, and I'm not having it anymore."

She was breathing hard by the time she finished her rant. Both Clara and Matilda were staring at her open-mouthed, and she felt her cheeks redden. She couldn't believe her own outburst. She rarely lost control like that, but she'd had beyond enough of Matilda treating Clara like garbage.

"Are you going to let her speak to me like that?" Matilda demanded woodenly. She seemed too stunned to react.

The few seconds waiting for Clara's response dragged on for a lifetime. Addie half expected Clara to throw her out. As much as Clara didn't like her aunt, family was family, and Addie had been unforgivably rude.

Instead, Clara shot Addie a look like she had just pulled her from a burning building. "Yes, I am. You're welcome back to my home whenever you can manage to be polite to my guests, but until then, I'll have to ask you to leave."

It was Addie's turn to stare. She couldn't believe Clara was taking her side over her aunt's.

Neither, it seemed, could Matilda. "Well, I *never*," she muttered, rising with a huff and storming away.

Clara and Addie looked at each other and giggled. "I can't believe you said that," Addie said, once she'd finally regained her composure.

"Me? What about you?" Clara said, laughing again. She bit her lip. "Did you really mean what you said? About me?"

Addie looked at the table and turned her cup around in its saucer, the china squeaking. Looking at Clara suddenly felt overwhelming. "Of course I did. It's all true."

"Thank you," Clara said quietly. "I suppose we both could have been nicer, but she's been asking for a good telling-off for years."

"I hate how much she belittles you. You deserve so much more,"

Addie said to her rotating coffee cup. Matilda wasn't the only one Clara deserved more from.

"I feel rather bad about it now, but it was quite satisfying to listen to. I should probably apologize to her. I might wait a week or two for her to calm down."

"I'm the one who should apologize. I'll write to her, if you think she'll even read a letter from me instead of burning it."

Clara put her hand on Addie's to stop her from spinning the cup. "You don't need to. You've nothing to apologize for. You were just standing up for me. Remember when I knighted you in the park? You were being my brave defender again."

Addie felt worse than she had when she'd been listening to Matilda harp at Clara. Her protection was worthless. She had wounded Clara far more deeply than Matilda ever had. "Thank you for defending me too. You didn't have to do that."

"I meant what I said too. She doesn't get to drop by uninvited and insult you. Anyway, I was thinking of going to the movies. Would you like to come?" Clara asked. "The theater downtown is playing *Frankenstein*. You always loved that novel."

"You remembered," Addie said, pleasantly surprised. She hesitated, not wanting to check her wallet in front of Clara. The Willoughby theater was pricier than some at thirty-five cents a ticket, and she wasn't sure if she would enough to pay her hardware store bill for the delivery she was expecting tomorrow.

"It'll be my treat," Clara said.

"Well, all right then," Addie said, and Clara grinned. Her heart leapt at the sight. It had been so long since that smile had come to Clara's lips so naturally. Addie hadn't seen the blond book club woman around again, but she wondered if that was the reason for Clara's good mood.

Clara brought the car out and opened the passenger door for Addie. Normally, it would have felt like a date, but Clara was clearly planning to go anyway, regardless of whether or not Addie came along. The invitation was obviously born of coincidence rather than deliberate choice.

By the end of the movie, Addie had tears coursing down her cheeks. The film made Dr. Frankenstein's creation more sympathetic, and his death at the hands of the angry villagers broke her heart.

"That was rather devastating," Clara said as they emerged into the lobby. Although her eyes appeared dry, she sounded like she had a head cold, and her damp handkerchief was crumpled up in her fist. "He was so lonely, and all he wanted was a friend."

Addie pressed the heels of her hands to her eyes to try to lessen her tears, but Clara's words only made her cry harder. She could barely see the doors as they walked outside, trying to stifle her sobs. She thought of those first lonely months in Topeka when she had felt so alone, rejected by her family and society, something unlovable and grotesque. Even worse, she had recognized those same feelings in Clara and had exploited them instead of offering her genuine friendship and love.

"I don't suppose you'd like to get a bite to eat since we're downto—oh, Addie, what's wrong?"

Addie shook her head, not trusting her voice. Clara shepherded her to the car, putting an arm around her as if to shield her from any curious onlookers. The thoughtfulness of the gesture only made her cry harder, much to Clara's obvious dismay.

"Oh dear," Clara said worriedly, casting a sideways glance at her before starting the car. "I knew the movie might be sad, but if I'd realized it would upset you this much, I would have suggested something else."

Addie's confusion was enough to distract her from her morbid thoughts for a moment. "That doesn't make sense. You were going to the movie anyway, whether I came or not."

Clara's eyes widened, and her hands tightened and untightened on the steering wheel a few times. "Um. Yes, that's right. Never mind, forget I said anything."

Addie still didn't understand, but Clara clearly didn't want to talk about it, so she did her the courtesy of letting it drop. At least the interruption had caused her crying to slow to a trickle.

"Here." Clara offered her a fresh handkerchief.

Addie accepted it gratefully, dabbing at her eyes and blowing her nose with a comically loud honking noise. She cringed with embarrassment.

Clara laughed beside her. "I didn't know there was a goose in the car."

"It's the latest in automotive security," Addie joked. She thought of their encounter with the angry goose in the Public Garden.

"You're always there when I need protection from wayward geese," Clara said with a smile.

Addie fiddled with Clara's handkerchief in her lap, then cleared her throat. "I know I haven't always been there for you when you needed me."

There was a long stretch of silence. She feared she had made a fatal error. Why had she brought up the past when they had been having a nice evening? Well, nice until she'd ruined it by blubbering all over the place over a silly movie.

"Let's not dwell on the past," Clara said at last. "We've both changed a lot since then. Anyway, what book would you like to see made into a film next?"

Addie gratefully seized on the change of topic, marveling at Clara's willingness to move on. If someone had betrayed her as she had Clara, she couldn't imagine ever forgiving them.

❖

"I guess this is good night," Addie said as Clara turned off the car, but she made no move to get out.

Neither did Clara, even though she knew she should. This was dangerous territory, and yet, she kept being drawn in deeper. Even after all that had passed between them, she half wished Addie would lean over and kiss her. The wisest move would be to bid Addie good night and shut herself away in the house, safe from any temptation.

"Would you like to come in for a nightcap?" Her mouth moved before her brain could catch up with it. The words hung in the air between them, more charged than the invitation should have warranted.

"I'm not sure if that's a good idea," Addie said at last. "I'd probably better not."

Clara knew she was right, but the rejection still stung. She infused false cheeriness into her voice as she said, "We'll have to arrange another visit for you and Pip some other time, then. He loves seeing you."

"Maybe I could come in for just a minute, to say good night to him," Addie said.

"He'll like that." Clara chose not to analyze the way her heart jumped at Addie changing her mind, even if it was just to see Pip.

As she unlocked the kitchen door, she realized that despite living on the property for months, Addie had never actually been inside the house. She looked around curiously, and Clara was glad she'd washed the dishes before going out instead of leaving them in the sink for later as she sometimes did.

Even though she had sought Addie out tonight and encouraged her to come inside, Clara felt distinctly awkward now that they were standing in her kitchen.

Apparently, Addie did too. She was looking at the cabinetry, the dish rack, the brand-new refrigerator, anything but Clara. "Where's Pip?"

"I leave him in his cage upstairs when I go out. I'll go get him."

Clara fled to the safety of her bedroom where Pip greeted her delightedly.

"Guess who's here?" she asked him as she opened the cage. He obligingly flew to her shoulder for the trip downstairs but abandoned her as soon as he caught sight of Addie.

"Hello, friend," she cooed at him, petting the top of his head with her finger.

Watching them, Clara felt like an outsider in her own home. She tried not to let self-pity overwhelm her as she realized that he liked Addie more, even though he was supposed to be *her* pet. She shouldn't leave Pip loose, but she wanted to retreat upstairs and lick her wounds in private.

More than anything, she needed Addie to leave. It was too tantalizing having her there, like a hot stove she desperately wanted to touch. Addie would surely burn her, but Clara kept being drawn inexorably closer. She had carefully planned bumping into Addie on her way to the movies, which gave her enough plausible deniability to save face. She knew the truth, though. Her resolve to keep her distance was slipping.

Even as she told herself she needed to call an end to the evening, Addie looked up at her.

"I miss you," Addie said. "I miss you terribly. I know I've no right to say so or to ask anything of you. You've already gone so far beyond what any reasonable person would do, but I needed you to know that."

Clara's pulse beat like a drum as she tried to formulate a response, but no words came.

"I'm sorry. I shouldn't have said that. I'll go now," Addie said.

She walked over to return Pip, avoiding Clara's gaze. As soon as he hopped from her shoulder to Clara's, she turned and hurried toward the door.

"Wait," Clara said, her voice finally working.

Addie turned back, hope blazing in her face.

"I'm glad you're here," Clara said quietly. "I…missed you too."

Addie's smile was bright enough to warm a house in December. "Good night, Clara."

"Good night," Clara said, grinning back.

Chapter Twenty-Seven

Addie was honest-to-goodness whistling as she worked the next day. She was more optimistic than she could remember being since before the Depression, and it had nothing to do with the nearly three dollars in tips she had earned already today. Even as she cleared one table, the bell over the door announced the arrival of more diners.

Her new customers were a woman and a boy who looked around seven years old. They both ordered the daily special, grilled cheese and tomato soup. As soon as Addie served them, she knew the boy was going to be trouble. Like a cat, he slowly pushed the bowl off the table without breaking eye contact with her. At the crash, his mother looked around in dismay.

"Oh, Timothy, what have you done this time?" she chastised him.

Timothy hung his head but smirked at Addie when his mother couldn't see. She mopped up the spilled soup and shattered bits of china, thankful that she didn't have children. As she started back to the kitchen, he stuck his leg out. She stumbled but managed to keep her footing.

When she returned to check on them after dessert, she found Timothy using his whipped cream to finger paint on the table. Her temper snapped, and she spoke before she could stop herself.

"Timothy, you listen to me," she said sternly. He stopped, looking startled. She remembered all the times she or her siblings had acted out and tried to channel her mother's authoritarian tone. "All of us in this restaurant are working hard to make food for people like you and your mother. Unless you'd like to come into the kitchen and cook or clean for us, you stop that immediately."

He wiped his finger on his napkin and meekly folded his hands in his lap. Addie doubted he was really contrite, but maybe he'd decided that being scolded by her was more annoying than whatever fun could be derived from causing more mischief.

"I'm Beth Nelson," the woman said.

Addie introduced herself in turn, wondering what this was about. Customers weren't generally in the habit of introducing themselves to their waitresses. She hoped Mrs. Nelson wasn't about to yell at her or get her in trouble for scolding her son.

"I don't suppose you have any experience as a nanny?" Mrs. Nelson asked.

Addie stared at her, too startled to consider lying. "No, I don't. Why do you ask?"

Mrs. Nelson heaved a sigh. "As you may have noticed, Timothy is a holy terror. I simply cannot hold on to a nanny for more than a few weeks, even in this economy. The last one quit after he put a snake in her bed. I put a request in with the agency, but they don't have any girls available whom he hasn't already driven away."

Addie glanced at Timothy, who was loading chocolate chips onto his spoon. She suspected he was intending to catapult them at an innocent bystander rather than eat them, but at her glare, he put them in his mouth and chewed insolently.

"You see, he listens to you," Mrs. Nelson said. "At least a little, which is more than I can say for the last few nannies. I'm desperate, I tell you. I'll pay you fifteen dollars a week, plus room and board."

"I'm sorry, but I'm not interested." While the money was tempting, there was Clara to consider. Their connection last night lingered in her mind and bolstered her hopes. Taking the job would mean moving out of the garage and keep her too busy to work on the garden or spend any time with Clara. If Clara liked having her around or there was the slightest chance she might even love her again someday, she wasn't going to risk leaving.

"Fine, how about twenty a week?" Mrs. Nelson said, apparently interpreting her refusal as a matter of salary.

Addie shook her head. "It's not a question of money. I have other reasons for staying where I am. I hope you find someone soon."

Mrs. Nelson sighed heavily. "Well, it was worth a try. We're leaving for the White Mountains next week, and I had really hoped to hire someone by then. Let me give you my card in case you change your mind."

Addie tucked the card into her apron pocket. She didn't intend to use it for herself, but perhaps Clara knew someone who was good with children and looking for work.

Later, Addie hummed to herself again as she harvested a few potatoes and ears of corn to have for supper. She hoped Clara would agree to join her. It was a humble meal, but she had spent Mrs. Nelson's generous tip at the grocer on a few ounces of real butter. Even Clara didn't make that splurge very often, usually sticking with margarine.

She didn't want to scare Clara away with the dinner invitation, but things had been going so well between the two of them that she thought it was worth the risk. Hopefully, Clara would see by her actions how much she'd changed and that she truly cared for her.

She rested the basket of vegetables on her hip as she walked toward the front of the house to ring the doorbell, still humming. The song died on her lips as she saw Clara escorting a stunningly pretty brunette up the walkway. She ducked back into the shadow of the house, but they were so engaged in conversation that she doubted they would have noticed her anyway. She wished she could hear what the stranger said to make Clara's face light up with laughter.

Blood pounded in her ears as Clara let the dark-haired girl into the house and closed the door behind them. The girl's red overcoat seemed burned into her retinas. Regret and sick, bitter jealousy rose in her gorge like bile. Clara didn't let just anyone into her house. Not even the book club blonde had gotten an invite. Clara must have been serious about this one.

Clara's bedroom window faced Addie's little garage room, and she shamelessly stared, looking for any sign of what Clara and her guest might be up to. She had no right to that information, nor any claim on Clara, but she felt the sting of betrayal nevertheless. If she was a better person, she would have wanted Clara to be happy. But if she was a better person, she probably would never have pursued Clara at all.

Clara's bedroom curtains stayed closed for nearly an hour, the sun slowly moving across the house. Addie had nearly given up watching when they flicked open. There was the mystery girl, naked as the day she was born, the sunlight highlighting every curve of her body. Addie could see movement behind her, presumably Clara, but she wrenched her own curtain closed, sick to her stomach. Now that she had confirmation of what she'd been suspecting, she no longer wanted to know anything more.

Addie barely tasted as she ate, the silky melted butter going unappreciated as she shoveled her food into her mouth. She couldn't shake the image of Clara's carefree grin, how comfortable she looked with the other woman. She stabbed a piece of potato with her fork, wishing it was Clara's new lover instead. Clara had seemed happier around Addie recently. She'd hoped it was because of Clara's softening feelings for her, but now she knew the truth.

What would Eva think about all of it? The worst part of losing her hadn't been losing her home or financial security. Eva had been the one person who truly knew her and hadn't turned away. Addie had been able to tell her everything, even the worst parts of herself, her selfishness, her fear, her opportunistic nature, and Eva had never once judged her for it.

Clara now knew her better than anyone ever had, perhaps even Eva. Clara was good-hearted and generous of spirit, willing to be Addie's friend after all that had passed between them, but she had decided to move on. Addie couldn't blame her, really. It was a smart decision. Whoever Clara's new lover was, Addie just hoped she knew what she had and treasured Clara as she herself should have.

Clara was too kind to kick her out onto the street, despite the awkwardness it might cause in her new relationship. Now Addie had the chance to repay that kindness in one small way, by leaving of her own accord and making it easier for Clara.

She walked to the payphone outside the filling station up the road and called Mrs. Nelson, who sounded almost in tears from relief that Addie had changed her mind. She confessed to both surprise and gratitude that Addie was willing to start right away, even that very night if the Nelsons wanted.

She had grown accustomed to moving every few months, and it took her only a few minutes to pack her minimal belongings. She didn't want to leave without saying good-bye, but she couldn't trust herself to actually go if she spoke to Clara in person. It would be too tempting to stay, when her departure was the best thing for Clara. She scribbled out a note instead, leaving it on the neatly rolled-up mattress.

Other than the note, she left the little room exactly as she'd found it three months ago. She stood in the doorway surveying it for a moment before she left, her heart heavy as she locked the door for the last time. She dropped the keys for the room and the garden shed in Clara's mailbox, resisting the urge to snoop around the house to see what Clara and her guest might be up to. She had a good enough idea already, and it would only make her jealousy worse.

❖

"Would you care for coffee or tea before we start?" Clara asked as she opened the door to her studio at the back of the house.

"No, thank you," Mary Banks said with a smile. "I'd just as soon not have to interrupt your work to answer the call of nature." She looked around the room with a professional eye, nodding in approval.

Clara knew her studio was probably smaller than the ones Mary was used to posing in, but she was proud of it nevertheless. It was a pity she hadn't been very inspired lately to put it to good use. Her father had suggested she focus on improving her technical skills while she waited for inspiration to return, hence hiring Mary.

Mary was so businesslike in how she shed her clothes that Clara didn't even blush when she settled on the chaise completely naked. Clara had her lie back with her arm over her head, resting on the back of the chaise. Her first few pencil marks were timid and clumsy, but she soon got into a rhythm. She focused on the lines of Mary's body, the way the muscles and bones underneath the skin shaped them. The hands were the hardest part. Her first attempt made Mary's fingers look like Lovecraftian horrors. She grimaced in dismay, not least because the thought made her remember in vivid detail Addie describing *The Call of Cthulhu* to her one night as they walked home from Rosie's. She erased her botched effort with a huff of frustration.

"The light's fading in here," Mary pointed out after a while. "Do you want to move to another room?"

Clara realized she was right. She could turn on some more lamps in the studio, but it wasn't nearly as good as natural light.

"Would my bedroom be all right? It's the only room on the other side of the house with something comfortable for you to sit on. But if it's too awkward…"

Mary laughed good-naturedly. "Don't worry about that. I've been doing this for long enough that posing in your bedroom isn't the least bit uncomfortable for me."

Mary opened the curtains while Clara moved the little bench from its usual position at the foot of her bed so Mary had somewhere to sit. Since her bedroom was upstairs and at the back of the house, there was no danger of any of her neighbors seeing inside.

After so many months of not being able to draw anything, she was immensely relieved to find the ability coming back to her. The new life blooming in the garden, her rekindled relationship with Addie, being able to create art once again…she could barely believe her good fortune.

As soon as Mary left, Clara bustled out in search of Addie. She was so pleased with how the drawing session had gone that she wanted to celebrate, and Addie was the first person she wanted to tell. She knew Addie had finished work several hours earlier, so she was most likely in the garden. It seemed like she was out there all the time now, the previously sparse yard now bursting with growth.

To her surprise, Addie was absent from the garden. She knocked on the door of her room but heard only silence. She wondered where Addie could be; she didn't usually socialize much, except sometimes with the girl from the hardware store. Clara wondered if Addie was with her, trying not to feel jealous at the thought.

Since Addie was nowhere to be found, she decided to go over to her family's house and share her excitement with them instead. It was such a nice day that she decided to walk instead of bothering with getting the car out. Before she left, she checked the mailbox. Resting on top of the handful of letters and catalogs that filled it were two keys. She frowned as she lifted them out, trying to figure out why they looked familiar. After a moment, she recognized them as her own, for the garden shed and for Addie's room.

She couldn't fathom how the keys had gotten into her mailbox. It couldn't possibly have happened accidentally, so Addie must have put them there. She riffled through the mail, but none of the letters or cards were from Addie with an explanation. She would have to go and see for herself.

Trepidation filled her as she climbed the garage stairs, her heart beating faster with each step. When she opened the door to Addie's room, she noticed at once how bare it was. Other than the lack of dust, there was no sign that Addie had ever been there. She looked around searchingly, as if Addie might be hiding under the cot or in the water closet.

Finally her eyes landed on an envelope lying on top of the rolled-up mattress. Her fingers trembled as she opened it and slid the letter out.

Dear Clara,

I can't tell you how much I appreciate your kindness and generosity in opening your home to me once again despite what has passed between us. Someone has offered me a promising opportunity, and I feel that taking it would be best for both of us. I will always think of you fondly, but the time has come for me to move on and allow us both to build lives of our own. Please tell Pip I love him and will miss him dearly. I wish you all the happiness in the world.

Best wishes,
Addie

Clara read it several times, the meaning of the words finally sinking in. She crumpled the paper in her hand, then rushed to smooth it out, running her fingers over Addie's handwriting.

That very morning, she had thought she and Addie were on the same page about rekindling their romance. How had it all gone wrong so quickly? Addie might have found another lover, maybe the hardware girl with her tanned arms and powerful truck. It didn't escape her notice that Addie only mentioned missing Pip, not her.

Addie must have truly changed if she was leaving now. She had to know that Clara was falling in love with her all over again, that Clara's fortune would be hers to enjoy if she simply sat back and waited. That she had left anyway could only mean that whatever affection she might have for Clara, it wasn't enough. Clara couldn't believe how foolish she had been to open her heart to Addie yet again.

At least this time, Addie hasn't led her on or made her believe she was anything more to her than a useful acquaintance. Clara had demanded Addie be honest with her, and she had. It wasn't Addie's fault if Clara didn't like what that honesty revealed. Even so, she felt abandoned and terribly alone.

CHAPTER TWENTY-EIGHT

Within a few days of working for the Nelsons, Addie understood why they'd gone through so many nannies. Timothy was as much of a menace as he'd seemed in the restaurant, and now she was subjected to his reign of terror for sixteen hours a day. If she'd had any alternative besides going back to the family that had rejected her, she would have quit too.

Even their upcoming vacation in the White Mountains wasn't as exciting as it should have been. Mr. and Mrs. Nelson wanted a break from Timothy as much as from work and housekeeping, and Addie would be expected to keep him occupied throughout the trip. She hoped there would be other children at the chic new resort where they'd be staying, along with all sorts of activities to make him too tired to cause mischief.

Thankfully, that hope turned out to be accurate. Within a few days of their arrival in New Hampshire, Timothy had fallen in with a group of other children. They happily spent the mornings plotting and the afternoons enacting the planned schemes, terrorizing guests and staff alike with their antics. Addie did what she could to mitigate the mischief, but even her commanding tone had its limits.

Mr. Nelson was called back to Boston on business partway through the trip, leaving Mrs. Nelson to turn to Addie for company instead. It was more like being a paid companion again instead of a nanny, but Addie certainly wasn't going to complain. She infinitely preferred listening to Mrs. Nelson gossip about the other guests to trying to wrangle Timothy all day.

"Some new guests are arriving today. They're also from

Willoughby, believe it or not. I don't know them terribly well, but this'll be a good opportunity to become better acquainted," Mrs. Nelson said over luncheon. "Oh look, here they are now."

Certainty and dread filled Addie in equal measure as she turned toward the doorway. She knew in her bones who it would be. Sure enough, Clara was standing there sandwiched between her two brothers, giving Addie a chance to observe how heartbreakingly lovely she looked. She was wearing a new dress in a pink floral pattern that went perfectly with her freshly dyed chestnut brown hair, a single strand of pearls around her neck.

She laughed at something Albert said, then looked around the dining room. Addie could tell the moment she spotted her. The smile slid from her face, and she stopped in her tracks, her body language stiff and unfriendly. She abruptly changed course and led the way to a vacant table on the opposite side of the dining room, her brothers and parents trailing behind her.

Her obvious dislike stung. Addie knew she had plenty to answer for as far as Clara was concerned, but she didn't think their last parting warranted such cold conduct. After all, she had left for Clara's own good. At worst, Clara should have felt slightly awkward about seeing her, but her look had been more of a glare. Addie resolved to steer clear of Clara as much as she could for the rest of her time at the lodge.

"How odd," Mrs. Nelson said, frowning slightly. "It looked like they were coming over here, but they veered off."

"Maybe they prefer the view over there. Timothy is going for a hike with the MacDonald family after lunch. Shall I go with them?" Addie asked, eager to turn the conversation away from the Coopers. She was desperate enough to avoid Clara that she was willing to tag along on the hike, something she otherwise would have avoided by any means necessary.

"I shouldn't think there'd be any need for you to go along," Mrs. Nelson said, still eyeing the Coopers. "Take the afternoon off and enjoy yourself. It'll do you good to get some relief from Timothy and spend time with young people your own age. He's the MacDonalds' problem for a few hours. Both of those young men who just came in are single and reasonably attractive, and they've recently become quite well off, I believe. Perhaps you could make their acquaintance."

Addie cringed at the suggestion. Both Albert and Fred would just as soon spit at her as marry her, she was certain. They were seated facing her and scowled in unison when they saw her looking at them. Clara sat between her parents with her back to Addie, no doubt by design. All the way from across the dining room, Addie could see the flush on the back of her neck. She was sitting ramrod straight, no longer the slouching and shy girl that Addie had met in France. It felt so long ago that it might have been another lifetime.

Over the next few days, it felt like Clara was shunning her. She couldn't understand why Clara was quite so upset with her. Maybe things hadn't turned out well with her new lover, and she was holding Addie to blame.

Whatever the reason, it was impossible not to notice the effort Clara was putting into avoiding her. At mealtimes, either Fred or Albie would enter the dining room solo; if he saw Addie, he immediately turned around and walked out again. The activities director at the resort tried to match Addie with the three Cooper siblings for tennis doubles, but when she tried to join them, they lost interest in playing and disappeared.

The last straw came after breakfast on the third day, when she felt Clara watching her from a lawn chair as she tried to coax Timothy to throw his horseshoes at the target rather than the other children. Deciding enough was enough, she abandoned her post and marched in Clara's direction. Clara practically leapt from her chair and scurried away before Addie could reach her.

"Clara, wait," Addie called, but Clara sped up. Once Clara made it inside the hotel, Addie gave up and headed back to the horseshoe area. There was no telling what Timothy might have gotten up to in her brief absence. As she passed Clara's abandoned chair, she realized that Clara had forgotten her sketchbook in her haste. Before she could stop herself, she scooped it up and opened it to a page at random.

She regretted it immediately. Whatever creative rut Clara had been in over the summer, she had clearly gotten over it. The drawing was unmistakably the dark-haired woman she had seen in Clara's room, sitting naked on a chair with the edge of a bed frame in view to the side. Sunlight streamed in the window behind her, making her look radiant. Addie wanted to tear it out and rip it to shreds.

Instead, she slammed the sketchbook shut and shoved it in her shoulder bag to return later, assuming she could get close enough to

Clara to do so. It was the perfect excuse to force Clara to speak to her, even if only in passing. She didn't want to look at the drawing anymore. There was a dull ache in her throat whenever she thought about it, so she tried not to.

Timothy ran her ragged for the rest of the afternoon, and it wasn't until nearly dinnertime that she remembered the sketchbook. She found Albie and Fred in the midst of a heated tennis match, but Clara was nowhere to be seen. Not wanting to interrupt their game, she returned to the lodge to see if Clara's parents knew where she was.

She caught sight of Clara's mother and Mrs. Nelson in the music room. They looked up in unison as she came in through the French window.

"Do you know where Clara is?" she asked.

"She left for a hike right after lunch. She wanted to paint the view from higher up the mountain. She's not back yet," Mrs. Cooper said. "And I must say, I'm getting a bit worried. At this rate, she'll miss dinner. Of course, she's so much like Daniel. She may well have simply lost track of time. Sometimes he forgets to come down for meals when he's painting."

"Yes, she does tend to do that," Addie said. "She left her sketchbook outside earlier. I was hoping to return it to her."

"I can give it to her if you'd like," Mrs. Cooper said, holding out a hand expectantly. She was behaving perfectly cordially, which led Addie to think that Clara must not have told her about whatever Addie had done to upset her.

Addie shook her head. "No, thank you. I'd prefer to give it to her myself."

"It looks like it might storm, doesn't it?" said Mrs. Nelson, craning her neck to look out the window at the dark gray clouds rolling in from the west.

Mrs. Cooper wrung her hands anxiously. "Oh no, she'll get absolutely soaked, and her painting will be ruined."

Mrs. Nelson patted her knee consolingly, then looked at Addie. "Miss Barnes, would you be a dear and go and fetch her? Maybe you can bring her in before the rain starts."

"Well," Addie said, "I don't know the mountain at all. I wouldn't even know where to look for her."

Mrs. Cooper's face brightened. "It's simple. She was going up the Hairpin Trail. It passes right in front of the lodge, you can't miss it. There's a scenic overlook about half a mile up. I'm sure that's where she'll be."

"I'd be glad to, but Timothy will be needing his bath soon," Addie said slowly, searching her mind desperately for some excuse.

"I'll take care of that myself," Mrs. Nelson said, waving the objection aside. "I'd much prefer you help put Mrs. Cooper's mind at ease."

Addie looked at Mrs. Nelson's calm but steely face and knew the battle was lost. There was nothing for it but to go to Clara, however angry her reception might be.

She made a last-ditch effort to avoid the task, stopping at Clara's room in case she had come back unnoticed by her mother. She rapped on the door and called out "Room service," pitching her voice slightly higher in case Clara recognized it and refused to respond. She pressed her ear to the door but heard only silence. She tried the door handle and found it unlocked.

It was obvious that Clara wasn't there. The bed was neatly made, and the bathroom door stood wide open. For the sake of thoroughness, Addie checked the wardrobe and under the bed, but even Clara wasn't quite that desperate to hide from her. She placed Clara's sketchbook on the writing desk as she left. She had no intention of hauling it up the mountain with her as she searched.

She stopped off in her room to retrieve her raincoat and umbrella. She checked her hair in the mirror and reached for her compact to touch up her makeup but tossed it aside. It wouldn't do anything to soften Clara's feelings toward her, and besides, after half a mile of hiking she was likely to become sweaty and disheveled anyway. Any powder she put on her face would simply melt off.

Mrs. Cooper was as good as her word, and Addie found the trail with ease. Although fairly gentle at first, the path rapidly got steeper and she started panting before long. The umbrella came in handy as a makeshift walking stick as she clambered over rocks and enormous tree roots crisscrossing the path. The trail earned its name, with countless hairpin turns as she ascended. The air felt heavy with unshed moisture. Whenever the rain did start, they would be in for a hell of a storm. The higher she got up the mountain, the colder it was. Despite the exertion, she shivered and pulled her raincoat tighter.

She thought she must have gone half a mile at least. Surely, Clara couldn't have made it much farther than this while laden with her easel and paints. A stitch was forming in her side, and she was starting to feel the slightest bit irritated with Clara. Of course she loved her art, but couldn't she be the slightest bit more considerate of others? She had to know her mother would be worrying about her. If she was angry about Addie being the one to come fetch her, it served her right for being so selfish.

Rather ironic for you *to be calling anyone else inconsiderate and selfish.*

Fortunately, she was soon distracted from her self-recriminations. The next hairpin turn in the trail revealed the overlook Mrs. Cooper had mentioned. On a clearer day, the view would have been spectacular indeed, with sweeping vistas of the rest of the Presidential Range. Now, though, all she could see was gray. The clouds had moved in faster than she expected, and the wind was whistling angrily. Rain started lashing the ground.

The view was nowhere to be seen, and neither was Clara. Addie cursed under her breath, growing annoyed again. At this point, she wanted to be done with the whole miserable errand and comfortably ensconced back in the lodge. She wondered if Clara could have gone back by some other route, but there was no other path nearby, and they couldn't possibly have passed each other on the trail without noticing.

The wind was howling now, whipping right through her coat and chilling her. Her teeth started chattering as she looked around for signs of where Clara could be. Maybe Mrs. Cooper had been wrong about Clara's intended destination, and this whole errand had been pointless. She had almost convinced herself that was the case when a small spot of orange caught her eye among the brown and green of the ground. She knelt and identified it as a splash of paint. Dabbing at it with her fingertip, she could tell it had barely dried. Nearby, she saw three divots in the dirt, perfectly spaced to have come from Clara's easel.

Irritation morphed into fear and gripped her heart at the sight. Clara had certainly been here, and there was no way she could have gone back to the safety of the lodge without Addie seeing her. That left only one option: she was still out on the mountain, at the mercy of the storm. The only way to go was up.

By the time it occurred to her that she could have gone for help rather than trying to find Clara herself, Addie had already returned to the trail and started climbing. It had taken her far longer than she'd expected just to get this far, and by the time she got back to the lodge and rounded up someone to help her look for Clara, it would be even more difficult.

Indeed, it felt ten times harder now than it had to get to the overlook. The trees were thin and small up here, stunted by the high winds that regularly assailed them. The air was cold enough that the rain turned to sleet. Her umbrella proved useless. After it flipped inside out three times, she stowed it away and went back to using it as a walking stick, afraid it would either be ripped out of her hands or turn into a parachute and send her sailing off the mountain.

She called Clara's name, but the wind instantly swallowed her voice. The only experience she could compare it to was during her childhood in Kansas, when a tornado had once passed by less than a quarter of a mile from her family's farmhouse. She felt even smaller and more powerless now; at least back then, it had only been her own safety at risk. The thought of Clara being out in this, possibly lost and frightened, was more chilling than the icy rain.

Nightfall was coming on quickly, and between the clouds and the sleet, she could barely see more than a few feet in front of her. She had no idea how she would find Clara in this. All she could do was continue to put one foot in front of the other and pray. To distract herself from her fear and misery, she tried to think like Clara. What would have caused her to continue climbing after painting at the overlook, rather than going back to the lodge?

Her first thought was *so she wouldn't have to see me*, but she dismissed it. Clara had any number of options for avoiding Addie, as she'd demonstrated over the past few days. The hotel had plenty of places where she could distance herself, or she could have simply stayed at the overlook for longer. No, there had to be some reason for it.

The Basilica in Lyon. The Eiffel Tower. Their top floor apartment in Boston. Clara loved views, the higher the better. However lovely the overlook was, she would want to see the view from the summit, to know she was as far up as she could possibly get. Even if she'd seen the storm moving in, she would probably have thought she'd have enough time to get up and back before it hit.

Certainty filled Addie all the way to her bones. Clara might have gotten lost in the storm on her way to or from the summit. Addie would continue up the trail until she found her or until she couldn't go any farther.

Energized by having a plan at last, she threw herself back into the climb. It was sheer misery, but she stayed focused on Clara, possibly lost or hurt and alone in this mess. Addie was her only chance.

CHAPTER TWENTY-NINE

D amn," Clara hissed, wincing as she tried to move her swollen ankle into a more comfortable position. She hoped it was merely sprained and not broken, although the difference between the two felt like the least of her concerns at the moment. Whatever the diagnosis, it rendered her utterly helpless. With any luck, it would get cold enough to numb the pain, and she could drag herself down the wretched mountain.

The speed with which the weather had turned shocked her. Although she'd heard about the legendary storms on Mount Washington, her mind had simply refused to accept that a September day could start off with balmy blue skies and end in gale force winds and snow at the peak.

Whether she accepted it or not, that was her present reality, and she recognized the severity of the danger she was in. She cursed her hubris at wanting to see the summit on her own. She should have waited until Albie and Fred could go with her, but she had been so eager to prove to herself that she could do it.

Except it wasn't really herself she wanted to impress, was it? Ever since she'd found Addie here with the Nelsons, Clara had been trying to demonstrate how little she cared. She didn't need anyone, least of all Addie. Addie wasn't cruel enough to laugh at Clara's current predicament, but she certainly wouldn't have been impressed.

With that glum thought, she turned her attention to her current predicament. Nightfall was coming on fast, and her teeth wouldn't stop chattering. Her wool coat was no match for the icy wind, but she bundled it around herself as best she could. Despite the discomfort, she felt the siren call of sleep. She shouldn't give in, but surely, a few minutes wouldn't hurt.

Clara...Clara...

She was back in their spacious bedroom in Boston. Addie had come in with breakfast on a tray to surprise her and was shaking her awake. They were going to eat as quickly as possible so they could spend the rest of the day in an endless cycle of making love, cuddling, and sleeping.

"Just a few more minutes," she mumbled. As eager as she was for all of it, she was still so tired.

"Clara, you need to wake up! You're freezing," Addie said more urgently.

Clara groaned, trying to hold on to sleep for just a bit longer. Why was the room so cold? They must have forgotten to close the windows. Pip wouldn't be at all pleased. And why was the mattress so hard all of a sudden?

Addie shook her again, and finally, she remembered where she was. She tried to stand, but pain radiated from her injured ankle. Her fingers and toes felt numb. She wished the numbness would extend up to her ankle, but she wasn't lucky enough for that.

"Here, darling," Addie said, putting an arm around her shoulders and helping her sit up. "What happened? Are you hurt?"

"I fell," Clara mumbled, leaning into Addie's warmth. Maybe she could use Addie as a pillow and sleep some more. She could barely keep her eyes open.

Sharp pain flashed across her cheek, and she realized Addie had slapped her. "What was that for?" she asked indignantly, a little more awake now.

"You mustn't sleep. With the snow and wind, you might not wake up again. Sit here while I try to make us a little shelter."

Addie's words filtered through the pain and exhaustion of Clara's mind and finally sank in. She was in deadly danger, and now Addie was there right along with her. She watched as Addie dug in the snow with her umbrella.

She wished she could help, but she would be more of a hindrance in her present state. Her easel, canvas, and paint case had gone tumbling down the mountain in her fall. She dug around in her pockets for anything that might be helpful, coming up with a matchbook from the lodge, her little diary, a pen, and a stray bit of string.

By the time she finished her inventory, Addie had created a shallow trench just wide enough for the two of them to lie down side by side. She helped Clara into it, then disappeared from view. Clara could hear branches snapping and a muttered curse before she reappeared, dragging several pine branches.

"We need some shelter from the wind," Addie panted, trying to prop the branches over the trench as a roof. The wind blew them down immediately, and Clara had the odd feeling of being buried in Christmas trees. Addie dug her out, wincing as sleet hit her eyes.

"Here, maybe this will help," Clara said, remembering the string she'd found in her pocket.

Her fingers were almost completely numb, and Addie took the string from her carefully, the wind trying to snatch it as it passed between their hands. Addie shoved the handle of her umbrella into the snow as deep as she could. The wind tore at it, but she draped the branches over it and used the string to tie them together in a makeshift lean-to that held fast.

They huddled up next to each other in their temporary shelter, their teeth chattering. Clara could still feel the storm buffeting them, but the umbrella and the branches provided some relief. At least the sleet and snow could no longer reach them. She started to nod off again, but Addie kept prodding her.

"You can't sleep, dearest. It's too dangerous. We'll have to keep each other awake."

"How did you find me?" Now that she was slightly more comfortable, it finally dawned on her how strange it was that Addie should be here.

Addie wrapped her arms around her to warm her. "Your mother was worried about you, so Mrs. Nelson asked me to look for you. When you weren't at the overlook anymore, I tried to think about where you'd go."

"I might've gotten lost and gone down the wrong trail. What made you come this way?" Clara asked. It might have been her fatigue-addled brain, but the question felt vitally important somehow.

Addie shed her raincoat and draped it over their bodies like a blanket. Even though Clara's clothes were wet and freezing, Addie pressed herself against her under the coat. Heat flowed from Addie's body to hers, not nearly enough for her to be truly warm but much better than before. She tucked her hands in her armpits to try to coax some feeling back into them.

"You're very good at directions," Addie said. "The storm hadn't hit yet when you left the overlook, so you wouldn't have gotten lost at that point. There's only the one path, and you'd have been able to see it. And you like views from up high. Remember in Lyon, when you told me you wished you were a bird?"

Clara smiled at the memory. It felt like a lifetime ago.

"Anyway, I realized you must have gone higher to try to get a better view. After that, it was only a question of catching up with you."

A wave of affection washed over Clara. Addie was one of the only people who knew her well enough to figure out exactly where she had gone and why. Whatever else had passed between them, Addie couldn't fake that.

As uncomfortable as the ground was, Clara was exhausted enough that she felt herself nodding off again. From Addie's slow and steady breathing next to her, she was in similar straits. It was Clara's turn to prod her awake.

"Hmm?" Addie said sleepily.

"You fell asleep, and then I almost did too," Clara said.

Addie sat up slightly, flinching as the wind rattled their flimsy, makeshift tent. "That won't do. I'm really worried that if we fall asleep, we won't wake up again."

"We'll have to find some way to keep each other awake. Can you think of a game or something? My head is too fuzzy to come up with anything."

"I've just thought of one I used to play with my family. Have you ever played the Minister's Cat?"

It rang a vague bell, but Clara couldn't place it. She was so very tired. If she could only sleep for a few minutes, perhaps she could think more clearly.

"Stay with me," Addie said in her ear.

Clara felt a flash of irritation. What gave Addie the right to tell her what to do? If she wanted to take a brief nap, it was none of Addie's concern, and yet, she wouldn't stop talking.

Addie refused to take the hint and kept speaking. "We go back and forth through the alphabet, describing the minister's cat. So I would say 'the minister's cat is an artistic cat,' and then you would say 'the minister's cat is a…' "

Clara tried to think of an adjective starting with B. It took a surprisingly long time, but finally, she muttered, "Bossy."

"The minister's cat is a creative cat," Addie said, squeezing her hand.

"The minister's cat is a deceptive cat," Clara replied.

Addie inhaled sharply before continuing the game. "The minister's cat is an effervescent cat."

The game continued, Clara producing hypocritical, lying, narcissistic, two-faced, and venomous. She could feel Addie reacting to each word, but she couldn't bring herself to stop. It was the closest she'd come to being able to vent the anger she'd bottled up from Addie leaving her. At least her resentment was helping her stay awake in the bitter cold. She ought to thank Addie for that much, at least.

By the time Clara hit the stumbling block of X, the game had served its function of keeping them awake but had lost its appeal. Each descriptor stung more than the last, and Addie regretted ever suggesting it in the first place. Even an innocent parlor game wasn't safe from the conflict between them.

"Let's try something else now," she said. "Do you know any games we could try?"

Clara rolled to face her, wincing as she moved her injured leg. They were mere inches apart, their bodies pressed together for warmth. And perhaps comfort too, although Addie didn't know how much solace Clara was deriving from her presence.

"I don't want to play games," Clara said fiercely. "I never did."

"Well, all right," Addie said, feeling defensive. "We can do something else if you'd rather."

"That's not what I'm talking about, and you know it."

Addie was growing more bewildered by the second. At least Clara seemed more alert now, if only because she was inexplicably furious. "I'm not being deliberately obtuse. I really don't know what you mean.

One moment you're insulting me via feline adjectives, and the next, you're shouting at me for God knows what reason."

Clara let out a disgusted huff. "You're hopeless. I thought you had changed, I really did. But I guess it never stopped being a game to you, did it?"

"What? *Oh.*" Realization finally dawned, and Addie understood what Clara was really getting at. At last they were making some sort of progress. "You, us, our relationship was never a game to me."

"Well, you could have fooled me. In fact, you did for quite some time."

Addie sighed. The bitterness had returned to Clara's voice, like they were right back where they had started. "You wouldn't have liked the real me."

"How am I supposed to know who 'the real you' is anyway and decide for myself if I like her or not?"

"Fine," Addie said. Clara hated her already. She had nothing left to lose, so she might as well be fully honest now. "I'm vain and petty and shallow, and I'm the only thing I care about. I used to get up before you and put makeup on because I thought you'd only like me if I looked pretty. I lied about my past because I was ashamed of it. I could tell you thought I was worldly and exotic when we met. A yokel from Kansas with two living parents who can't stand the sight of her is a lot less appealing, isn't it? I knew you'd be devastated if you found out the truth, but I was more afraid of losing my comfortable home than of hurting you."

Clara didn't speak after she finished her diatribe, and Addie felt compelled to fill the silence.

"That's who I am," Addie said, wincing. "It's not a pretty picture, is it? But now you know all of me, even the parts I'd rather keep hidden."

She dreaded what Clara might say in response. She couldn't bear to hear that what little respect Clara had regained for her had slipped away. Hopefully, she had redeemed herself somewhat in Clara's eyes by coming to find her, and when they parted, Clara would hold on to more memories than just the bad ones.

"Why did you leave?"

The question took her by surprise, but maybe it shouldn't have. After all, Clara wouldn't expect her to do something for selfless reasons. Addie didn't have a particularly good history with her in that department. "I thought it would be easier on you, not having me around. You probably would have felt bad about evicting me, but I'm sure it was awkward with your new lady friend for me to be living there."

Clara's brow furrowed. "Who?"

"Your new…you know. Companion or whatever you want to call her."

Clara started to prop herself up on her elbow but hissed and lay down again. Every movement seemed to hurt her injured ankle. "I don't know what you're talking about. I haven't been seeing anyone."

"You needn't bother lying. You have every right to see whoever you want. Besides, I saw her," Addie said. It frustrated her that Clara wouldn't just admit it.

"Well, either you need your head examined or you've been to one too many seances and seen a ghost," Clara said tartly. "I'm not lying. When did you allegedly see this mystery woman?"

Addie was growing more confused by the second. "The day I left. I didn't imagine her, and she wasn't a ghost. I saw you talking to her, and I saw her in your bedroom. She had dark hair, and I'd describe her clothing, except she wasn't wearing any."

Suddenly, Clara was laughing. "Oh dear. Of all the luck. That wasn't what it looked like. That was just Mary."

"And Mary is…" Addie prompted. It was hard to conceive how she could have interpreted the situation wrongly, but Clara was still giggling as if it was the funniest error in the world.

"A model," Clara said, her laughter finally dying away. "An artist's model. She poses nude for life drawing classes and the like."

That certainly changed things, but Addie still had questions. "If you were just drawing her, why was she in your bedroom?"

"For the light," Clara said, the word *obviously* unspoken but implied. "We started in the studio, but after the sun started setting, we went to my room instead. There was no…funny business going on."

It was Addie's turn to laugh, both at Clara's prim wording and at the relief flooding through her. "And here I thought you had become quite the lady-killer."

"No," Clara said, suddenly serious. "I wanted to move on, you know. I tried seeing a few other women, but none of them were you."

Addie's breath caught. "It was the same for me. All I wanted was to make it up to you, but I didn't know how."

"I don't think you can. It's not an equation of 'you caused X amount of damage, so you must do Y to make up for it.' Love doesn't work that way."

"So how does it work, then?" Addie asked bluntly. It wasn't smooth or coy or clever, any of the things she'd always tried to be, but she cared too much about Clara's answer to worry about that.

"Hell if I know," Clara said, and they both giggled. "I don't suppose anyone knows, really. How do *you* think it works?"

Addie didn't think, just blurted out the first thing that came to mind. "All I know is that my life is better with you in it."

"Do you really mean that?"

Addie winced. It was painful that Clara had to ask, but it was a fair question. "I do. All I want is to be with you again. No gifts or charge accounts or fancy apartments, just you. I'll move back into your garage and dedicate all my time to showing you how much I care."

The seconds before Clara responded felt like a lifetime. Addie's words hung in the air between them like a physical presence. She wished she could take them back and lessen her vulnerability somewhat, but it was too late. All she could do was wait for Clara to decide her fate.

"First of all, that sounds exhausting to have you fussing over me all the time. You need a hobby or something," Clara said. "And secondly, don't you think you'd be much more comfortable in the house with me?"

"So you'll have me?" Addie said, hardly daring to hope.

"Yes, but If I'm to love you without reservation, I have a condition," Clara said sternly.

Addie's heart sank. She had known it was too good to be true, but she had allowed herself to hope. "What's your condition?"

"Total honesty from here on out," Clara said. "The things you've lied to me about, those were to make me feel better or to think more highly of you. To hide yourself from me. But I can't truly love you if I don't know you."

Addie swallowed hard. It was a reasonable demand, given their history, but it was more terrifying than if Clara had asked her to parachute off the mountain or defeat a bear in hand-to-hand combat. Still, Clara was giving her a chance, which was more than she deserved.

"I'll try. I'm not sure I know how to do that, though," she admitted.

She could hear the smile in Clara's voice as she said, "Well, there you go, you're starting off on the right foot already. It's all right not to know at first. How about this? Whenever your instinct is to lie to me, don't. It's probably something I'd particularly want to know."

Addie considered the suggestion. It was probably a good one, considering her record with Clara. "Are you sure you want one hundred percent honesty all the time? Not even the occasional white lie?"

"No white lies," Clara said, shaking her head. "Otherwise, you'll convince yourself not to tell me things to spare my feelings when really, it's just keeping me at arm's length."

"In that case, I ought to tell you that you have an awful singing voice."

Clara swatted her on the shoulder, laughing. "I didn't ask about that, thank you very much."

Addie held Clara close and smothered her cheeks with kisses. The gesture felt wildly insufficient to express the depth of her feelings, but she was limited in what she could do, given the circumstances. Clara's skin was ice-cold under her lips, reminding her how perilous their present situation was. They were still at risk of frostbite, hypothermia, or even death.

Even with that knowledge, exhaustion was encroaching, trying to convince her that there was no harm in taking a short nap. She and Clara forced themselves to stay awake using every method they could devise. They tried to play I Spy, but it didn't work very well when they were in near-total darkness. There wasn't much to spy in their little shelter besides each other, anyway. They tested their memories, rattling off the capitals of all forty-eight states and every country they could think of.

The hours crept by torturously slowly. Every so often, they would light one of Clara's matches to check the time on Addie's watch before the wind snuffed it out. It seemed to instantly find every minute crack in the walls of their shelter, reminding them of its ever-present power. When they got down to only a few matches left, they decided to save them for the morning. They clearly needed to stay hunkered down for the night, and who knew how long it would take them to find help? Besides, the brief flashes of light and warmth served to taunt them with reminders of how uncomfortable they were right now.

Addie lost all sense of time as the night wore on. She or Clara would fall silent for what felt simultaneously like seconds and eons. Dimly, she understood that they were freezing to death. It was too bad, but there were worse ways to go than cocooned with the woman she loved. She had done many things of which she was ashamed, but coming for Clara was something she could be proud of. Earning Clara's love, trust, and forgiveness was worth more than anything else she had done in her insignificant life.

Chapter Thirty

By the time they dug themselves out of their makeshift den, the sun had fully risen, and it must have been well into the morning. Clara had lost all sense of time over the past eighteen hours. With the sun shining and Addie by her side once more, her situation no longer seemed so dire. How could she possibly be in harm's way on such a beautiful morning? Pure, unmarred snow coated everything in sight, the sunlight sparkling off it like diamonds.

It looked like the perfect winter's day, but she was forced to acknowledge that the danger wasn't over. Addie found her a large branch to use as a crutch, but even with both the branch and Addie's help, she couldn't go more than a few feet before the pain in her ankle forced her to stop. It was obvious she was in no condition to descend the mountain under her own power.

"I won't leave you," Addie said as soon as Clara mentioned it.

"It's not as if you're leaving me forever," Clara said patiently. "It'll be just long enough for you to fetch help. At the rate I'm going, we won't reach the lodge until spring."

Addie put up a fight but was powerless to overcome Clara's stubborn insistence that her plan was the only reasonable option.

"Fine, you win," Addie said at last, throwing up her hands in exasperation. "Don't you dare go and die on me, do you hear me? Now that I've finally gotten you back, I don't intend to let you go that easily."

"It'll take more than a little cold to take me out," Clara assured her.

In truth, she was anxious about how she would fare without Addie's company and body heat to keep her warm, but she kept it to herself. It had been hard enough to convince Addie to go in the first place. Addie insisted on leaving her hat and mittens with Clara and had to be argued with to agree to take her raincoat. She shoved her hands deep into its pockets and set out, turning back to look at Clara every few steps until she was out of sight.

The sound of Addie struggling through the snow quickly faded, and Clara was aware of how terribly alone and vulnerable she was. Were the bears hibernating yet? Black bears didn't usually attack people, but if one came across her, injured and helpless, it might consider her an easy meal. Or if Addie lost track of where she'd been and couldn't lead the rescuers to her...

The thought of Addie coming back for her bolstered her spirits and calmed her whirring mind. She mustn't get hysterical. Instead, she focused on all she wanted to do once she was back at home. A million and one potential art projects were forming in her head, and she pulled out her diary to jot them down.

Between the chill and the thick wool mittens encasing her hands, her writing was barely legible, but she thought she'd be able to decipher the scribblings later. She smiled as she realized that these were the very mittens Addie had been knitting on the boat two years ago. How far they both had come since then.

They would need to find a new place to live. She didn't want to stay in the Willoughby house where she had spent so many months marinating in bitterness. She missed the city. There might be a vacancy in their old building, but would they really want to return there? It was probably better to start over somewhere with a clean slate, forge a real relationship based on openness and trust.

She'd asked Addie for total honesty, but she couldn't let herself off the hook. She needed to put in the effort to learn to trust Addie again, or else she'd wind up holding Addie's past against her without even intending to. She was no longer that shy, naive girl enthralled by someone she barely knew. She could stand up for herself, and she could also fight for their love. She and Addie should be each other's oases, not sources of suspicion or strife. The outside world was harsh enough for people like them without making it worse for each other.

The time dragged on as she waited for rescue. She tried to estimate how long it would take Addie to reach the lodge through the snow, find help, and then, for the rescuers to locate her. When they were first together, she'd only seen Addie's exterior, beautiful and obliging and endlessly graceful. She hadn't understood the iron will that ran beneath it. Nothing yet had been a match for Addie's unwavering determination to overcome any obstacle in her path, from being forced out of her home as a teenager to all the hardships of the Depression. That relentlessness drive for security had probably been what led Addie to lie to her in the first place, but it had its benefits too. She knew that Addie was determined enough that she would pull Clara down the mountain in a sled by herself if that was what it took.

There wasn't a trace of doubt in her mind that she would soon be safe. Until then, she would put all of her trust in Addie and wait.

Addie moved so quickly down the mountain that she thought her heart might burst out of her chest. She was struggling to catch her breath, and her leg muscles were screaming in agony, but every time she wanted to stop, she thought of Clara waiting patiently alone in their frigid, makeshift shelter. Clara was counting on her to bring help as quickly as possible.

As she drew close to the lodge, now teetering from exhaustion, she heard voices. She tried to call out, but she was gulping down air too desperately to be able to make enough sound to be heard. She forced herself to stumble toward the noise, hoping it hadn't been a hallucination. To her enormous relief, she turned a corner in the trail to find Fred and Albie leading a group of men bundled up against the frigid weather. They raced toward her as soon as she came into view.

"Where's Clara?" Fred demanded.

She pointed up the mountain, still too winded to speak. Finally, she choked down enough air to say, "She's all right."

"What happened?" one of the others asked. She recognized him as one of the groundskeepers from the hotel. It looked like Clara's brothers had rounded up everyone they could find for a search party.

"Hurt her ankle," she gasped, massaging a stitch in her side. "Up above the tree line."

In fits and starts, she managed to tell them approximately where Clara was and how to find her amid the mess from the storm. The group trooped past her, several of them bearing a canvas stretcher on its side.

She watched them disappear around the corner, wishing she could go with them. Instead, she trudged the remaining few hundred feet to the lodge. There was no snow at this lower altitude, but her legs ached, and her feet felt like they were made of lead. In her current condition, she would only slow the rescuers down. The important thing now was to get Clara to safety as quickly as possible.

Clara's parents were waiting anxiously in the lobby and descended on her the moment she entered. Addie told them what happened as briefly as she could. She longed for a hot bath and a bite to eat, but she sympathized with the Coopers' distress. Mr. Cooper went off to telephone the state police, who had been informed of Clara's disappearance.

Once she knew Clara was safe, Mrs. Cooper seemed to transfer her maternal instincts to Addie, ushering her to a chair by the huge fireplace in the lounge and plying her with cups of hot coffee and a plate of cookies.

"To think she was out there all night," Mrs. Cooper said tremulously, dabbing at her eyes with her handkerchief. "My poor girl. And you stayed with her, even though things have soured between the two of you. Why?"

Addie stared at her, taken aback by the bluntness of the question. She took a moment to gather her thoughts. "I couldn't leave her there by herself," she said at last. "No matter how upset she might have been with me, she was hurt and alone, and she needed me."

Although her eyes were still shiny with tears of worry, Mrs. Cooper looked at her shrewdly. "I'm not as clueless as you all think, you know. I'm aware that you and Clara had a...*special* friendship."

"I..." Addie couldn't speak. Terror flooded through her as she remembered the fights with her parents, her mother screaming at her for being "unnatural," her desperate exodus in the middle of the night. She had met that challenge and survived, had overcome every other challenge life had put in her path, but with just a few words, she was back to being that frightened eighteen-year-old.

Mrs. Cooper patted her hand. "Calm yourself, my dear. I won't deny that it disturbed me at first, but it's Clara's life to lead as she sees fit. It isn't the life I would choose for my daughter, but that choice isn't mine to make."

Addie gulped. Her heart was still thumping in her throat, but it slowed a little as the meaning of Mrs. Cooper's words filtered through her brain. Mrs. Cooper might not have been happy, but at least she wasn't rejecting Clara outright.

"I love her," she said at last. It felt freeing to say aloud, to admit it to someone else without hesitancy or deliberation.

"She was devastated when you left," Mrs. Cooper said quietly. "Two years ago, I mean. I don't know what happened, but it absolutely crushed her. I never want to see her in that much pain again. If you make her happy, that's good enough for me."

Addie was grateful to Clara for not revealing her deception to her mother. Mrs. Cooper's obvious maternal devotion moved her. Even though she didn't understand her daughter's life, she cared more about her happiness than about her following some prescribed formula for social acceptance. Impulsively, she grabbed Mrs. Cooper's hands.

"Make sure you tell Clara that," she said. "She needs to hear it from you, that her mother accepts her."

Mrs. Cooper smiled and squeezed Addie's hands. "I will. From what Clara's said, I gather you can't say the same. In that case, I hope you'll allow me to be embarrassingly cloying and love you unconditionally."

A lump formed in Addie's throat. She nodded, afraid she would cry if she spoke. She was spared from trying to talk while keeping her composure by the sound of voices coming from the front hall. Clara had returned.

CHAPTER THIRTY-ONE

As the stretcher jounced and jostled down the trail, Clara tried to remember the night before. The details were hazy, but she was fairly sure she had the gist of it. She only hoped none of her memories were hallucinations brought on by hypothermia. She was anxious to see Addie again as soon as she got back to the lodge, but the closer they got, the more nervous she became. What if their reconnection had been fueled by the dramatic circumstances and didn't hold up in the light of day?

She was still shivering underneath the mountain of wool blankets Albie had piled onto her, but she had to wipe her sweaty palms on her skirt as they reached the lodge. Her parents raced to meet her, both of them wiping away tears of relief. She embraced them as well as she could from the stretcher, trying not to move her ankle.

Her rescuers carried the stretcher into her suite and helped her onto the sofa, where a doctor examined her and pronounced her out of danger of frostbite or hypothermia but ordered her to go to the hospital to have her ankle X-rayed, as he suspected it was broken.

After the doctor left, her family clustered around her, fussing over her. Her mother kept plumping her pillows, her brothers kept offering to bring her things, and her father clung to her hands as if afraid she would run away if he released her. She knew they all meant well, but there was only one person she really wanted to see.

"Where's Addie?"

"Oh, of course," her mother said. "Just a moment. You boys, shoo. Yes, you too, Daniel. Fetch Miss Barnes and tell her she can come in now."

Once the male members of the family were gone, her mother took her father's place and squeezed her hands. "Addie and I had a nice talk while we waited for them to bring you back. I don't know what your plans are now, but I do know that girl adores you."

Clara stared at her. "Mother, do you mean...I mean, do you know?"

"Yes," her mother said. "I don't pretend to understand it fully, but all I care about is seeing you happy and secure. Your grandfather took care of the security. The happiness is up to you."

Clara beamed, too overwhelmed to speak. She hadn't realized how much she craved her mother's approval until she had it, but her relief was palpable.

There was a gentle tapping at the door, and a moment later, Addie walked in. She crossed the room hesitantly, a bouquet of asters from the hotel garden in her hand.

"I'll leave you two alone," Clara's mother said. She kissed Clara on the forehead, then patted Addie's shoulder as she passed. The silence echoed as the door closed behind her.

Their sleepless night had taken its toll on Addie, and up close, Clara could see how haggard she looked. She had obviously not changed her clothes or put on makeup since her return. She stood over Clara awkwardly, not speaking.

"Are those for me?" Clara prompted, gesturing at the flowers.

"Oh, of course. I forgot I was holding them. How silly of me," Addie said. She handed them to Clara. "How are you feeling?"

"Much better, thank you. It still hurts, but the doctor gave me some medication that's helping."

"I'm glad to hear it," Addie said.

"Are you well? No frostbite or anything?"

"Yes, I'm perfectly fine."

They were both being stiff and formal, and Clara hated it. As if reading her thoughts, Addie dropped to her knees beside her.

"I promised to be honest, so I'll just say what I'm feeling, regardless of the consequences. Did you really mean it, that you'd give me another chance?"

"Of course I meant it," Clara said, taken aback that Addie even needed to ask.

"And you still feel that way, even now that we're not on the brink of death? Everything you said last night is still true?" There was an urgency in Addie's tone that told Clara she was serious, that she genuinely feared that Clara might have changed her mind.

"Yes," Clara said, drinking in the pure joy that spread across Addie's face. "Except for one thing. I thought about it while I was waiting, and I don't think you should move back into the house."

"Oh," Addie said. "You're not ready for that yet, of course. I understand."

"That's not what I meant," Clara said. She had wanted to toy with Addie a little, but she was unwilling to leave her hanging any longer. "I think we should get a new house, one we choose together. We'll fill it with new memories. It'll be both of ours, not just mine. We need a clean break from the past. Deal?"

"You tease. You really had me worried there," Addie said, beaming. "Yes, it's a deal. You're stuck with me for as long as you'll have me."

Clara surged forward, ignoring the twinge in her ankle, and cupped Addie's face in her hands. "How about forever?"

"Forever sounds good to me," Addie said and kissed her.

"I'm home," Clara called.

Addie set down the copy of Clarence Darrow's new autobiography she had been reading and hurried into the hallway, Pip on her shoulder. It had been six months since their harrowing escape in the mountains, and she still got anxious if Clara was gone longer than expected. She took Clara's hat and placed it neatly on the rack in the hall closet as Clara hung up her coat.

"How did your top-secret errand go?" she asked.

"Very well," Clara said smugly.

When she didn't elaborate, Addie said, "You're an international woman of mystery, Clara Cooper. Have you turned into a spy?"

Clara laughed and tugged her by the hand back into the sitting room. "If I were, I couldn't tell you. No, it's something much better than that."

They sat on the couch, and Clara handed her a piece of official-looking paper.

"What's this?" Addie asked, bewildered.

"Read it," Clara said, gesturing at it and watching her face.

It was an account statement from the First National Bank of Boston stating that Adeline Barnes now had a net worth of one hundred thousand dollars.

"I don't understand," Addie whispered.

"It's simple," Clara said. "With that money, you can afford to live independently. Maybe not in glamorous luxury, but if you're careful and invest it wisely, you'll no longer be financially reliant on me. It's yours, free and clear, no matter what happens between us."

Addie stared at her, dumbstruck. Her mind couldn't get a firm grip on what Clara was saying, like a record spinning endlessly after the song had finished. She wondered if this was how Clara had felt when she'd found out about her inheritance. She glanced at the paper in her hand again, then let it flutter to the end table beside her.

"Why?" she finally managed to croak.

Clara smiled and squeezed her hand. "Because now you have no reason to stay with me unless you want to."

Addie decided it was a reasonable thought, given their history. Another question popped into her head. "But can you afford this, after the crash and everything?"

Clara nodded. "Yes, it's perfectly fine. My accountant wasn't too pleased, but most of my investments are in treasury bonds and weren't affected, and the others are slowly rebounding. I'll still be very comfortable."

"'Comfortable' is what rich people say when they don't want to call themselves rich," Addie said with a snort. "Trust me, I've met enough of them to know."

"Fine then, I'll still be *rich*," Clara said, giggling. "The point is to put us on more equal footing. I know you haven't always felt like you could be honest with me about yourself, or you thought you needed to impress me for me to want to be with you. That's not the case, but now you have a safety net anyway."

That was an aspect that Addie hadn't even considered. "Watch out, I'll completely let myself go now," she warned.

"Good, that means you feel safe to be yourself around me," Clara said, unshakingly positive. "Although even after you spent a sleepless night cowering under an umbrella on Mount Washington, you looked beautiful."

Addie kissed the back of Clara's hand, not quite believing her but overwhelmed by affection. "Whatever would I do without you?"

"I wonder that myself all the time," Clara said with mock seriousness.

"I don't even like to think about it," Addie said, shaking her head to chase the thought away.

She was grateful for the money, of course, which gave her the security she had always wanted. But more than that, Clara would never have to doubt her love again. That meant more than all the money and cars and fur coats she could ever have. She finally had a true home.

EPILOGUE

"We ought to go in and dress for dinner. Do I look all right?" Clara asked.

"You look beautiful," Addie said with a smile. Her straw hat was still covering her eyes as she lay back in her chair on their private deck.

Clara swatted her arm playfully. "You didn't even look at me."

"I didn't need to," Addie said, sitting up and turning toward Clara. Her eyes confirmed what she had already known. Clara's hair was a rich chocolate brown at the moment. She would probably change the color again soon, but whatever she went to next, Addie would love just as much. One curl had come unpinned, a few drops of green paint were smeared on her cheek, and the tip of her nose was starting to turn pink with sunburn. Addie didn't think she had ever looked so beautiful.

Clara had braved seasickness again for their month-long tour of Italy. In private, they called it their honeymoon, and that was what it felt like. Every morning they woke up alongside each other, ready to explore a new beautiful sight or simply enjoy the day together. Addie felt almost guilty for how happy she was, like she was getting away with some kind of con.

"What are you thinking?" Clara asked, rolling in her chair to face her.

Addie caressed her cheek with the back of her index finger. "That I don't deserve you."

Clara leaned into her touch. "I'm the only one who gets to decide that."

"And what's your decision?"

Clara frowned in pretend concentration. "Hmm. I think…yes."

"I hate to argue with you, but I'm not sure you're right," Addie said.

"No, we'd better not argue. We'll have less time together once we're back. I want to enjoy this time together," Clara said, serious again.

Shortly after their return in September, Addie would be starting a library science program at Willoughby College. Although she didn't need the money, she thought it would do her good to have something productive and helpful to devote her time to. She was nervous about returning to school after such a long time, but Clara believed in her so utterly that it was impossible not to feel bolstered by it.

Between her studies and working in the small garden of their new house in Boston, she wouldn't be able to spend nearly as much time with Clara as she had in the past. As much as she dreaded that aspect, she thought it would do them both good. Working toward a career would give her a sense of purpose and a feeling of security, even if she didn't need the money.

She pulled Clara to her feet, and they went inside, but they didn't make much progress in getting ready for dinner. Clara looked so enticing that Addie couldn't help but kiss her, gently at first but gradually increasing in intensity. Finally, they broke apart, both breathing heavily.

"Shall we go to dinner now?" Addie asked at last.

"Yes, but you're buying," Clara said.

"Who's the kept woman now?" Addie teased, basking in the warmth of Clara's laugh. Even a few months ago, raising the topic would have been unthinkable; now it was something they could joke about.

She wondered what other jokes they would develop years down the road. Thoughts of the future no longer frightened her. Instead, she felt hopeful, even excited. She wanted to see the whole world with Clara but also stay at home alone with her and soak in each other's company, forgetting anyone else even existed.

"On second thought, there's no need to rush to dinner. We have some time before we need to go…" Clara said, untying her robe.

"I wonder how we should fill the time," Addie said, pretending to ponder.

"I'm sure we can think of something." Clara's robe fell open as she lay down, giving Addie the tantalizing view of the curves of her hips and thighs.

Addie's mouth went dry at the sight, and she gave up all pretense. "I like the way you think," she said, her voice coming out as a husky rasp.

She leapt onto the bed. They both laughed as the impact sent Clara bouncing into the air. Addie stroked Clara's cheek and pressed their foreheads together.

"I love you so much," she whispered, tugging at Clara's robe to reveal her shoulder.

Clara smiled against her mouth. "I love you too."

Addie helped Clara fully remove her robe, then let Clara undress her. The tenderness with which Clara unbuttoned her blouse, carefully setting it on the chair next to the bed instead of tossing it on the floor, nearly took her breath away. Once she was naked, she clutched Clara against her, not wanting even a millimeter of space between them. Clara's skin against hers felt *right*, a bond that kept its purity even as they kissed passionately.

Clara moaned into her mouth, increasing Addie's desperate desire. She pushed Clara onto her back and lowered herself on top of her, still kissing her feverishly. Clara lightly scratched her nails down Addie's back, urging her on. Addie moved her fingers between Clara's legs, finding her wet and ready for her.

Gently, Addie eased two fingers inside her, drinking in the look of mingled ecstasy and love on her face. Clara gasped as Addie slid her fingers in and out, her body gripping tightly at them on each thrust. Addie would have been content to go on caressing Clara from the inside for as long as her wrist strength held out, but before long, Clara was stifling her cries into Addie's shoulder as she came.

"Never mind dinner, let's stay here forever," Clara murmured. "And maybe do that a few hundred more times."

"That good, hmm?" Addie teased.

"Oh, hush. You're getting impossibly smug," Clara said playfully.

Addie rested her head on Clara's chest, listening to the rapid thump of her heartbeat finally return to its normal sedate pace. She wondered how soon she'd be able to make it speed up again. Although she still felt a desire for her own pleasure, her focus was entirely on Clara.

Apparently, Clara had other plans. She rolled onto her side to kiss Addie, then moved down her body and carefully but firmly pushed her legs apart. Clara, once so timid both in and out of bed, quickly reduced

Addie's body to jelly and emptied her mind of all thought. Nothing mattered but Clara, her tongue working magic and her clever fingers eliciting gasps as they tweaked Addie's nipples. Addie grasped blindly for one of Clara's hands, threading their fingers together and squeezing as her climax ripped through her. Her ears rang from the force of it.

"Come here," Addie murmured once the rippling aftershocks finally died down.

She patted the bed beside her, and Clara obligingly moved. They lay there with bodies intertwined, utterly content. Clara traced aimless patterns onto Addie's skin, as if she was a canvas waiting to be adorned. Addie relished the warmth and softness of her touch. If she were a cat, she would undoubtedly have been purring.

"Can I draw you?" Clara whispered.

Addie groaned as Clara stopped caressing her, but she nodded. "If you must."

"This might mean missing dinner," Clara warned as she pulled out her sketchbook and pencils.

"That's no trouble. A missed meal isn't going to kill me," Addie said. When Clara felt so compelled to draw all of a sudden, Addie was happy to oblige her.

Addie dutifully adjusted herself according to Clara's direction, one arm raised above her head with the fingers arranged just so, the other draped across her stomach. She watched fondly as Clara extinguished the electric lights and lit the old-fashioned kerosene lamp instead, moving it around until it cast the perfect glow on Addie's skin.

The dimmer light made her sleepy, and she remembered the drawing Clara had done of her in the lavender field two years ago. She allowed herself to drift in and out of a light doze, the scratching of Clara's pencil or the sound of a car horn through the open window occasionally rousing her.

"There," Clara said at last. She turned it around so Addie could see.

Addie gasped. "It's beautiful."

"It is rather, isn't it? If I do say so myself," Clara said.

It wasn't as polished or neat as Clara's work usually was, but Addie thought it depicted her essence more than any drawing Clara had done of her before. It wasn't idealized, just Addie as she was: barefaced, her hair mussed, a few freckles from spending so much time in the sun. Despite that, she didn't feel self-conscious about being captured looking less than her best. It was impossible when she could feel Clara's love for her radiating off the page.

Addie couldn't think of words that were adequate to express the depth of what she was feeling: gratitude for Clara's forgiveness and love, the comfort and security Clara had given her, the sheer joy she felt doing simple daily tasks with Clara by her side. She tugged Clara into her arms and squeezed, hoping that was enough to communicate her thoughts.

It seemed to be. Clara's eyes were shining brightly when Addie finally released her. They sat there smiling at each other until Addie's stomach let out a loud grumble. Clara snickered.

"You're the one who made me skip dinner," Addie protested.

Clara waved that aside. "Being the muse of a genius isn't all sunshine and rainbows, you know. Missing a meal is a small price to pay for me to create my masterpiece."

Her case was weakened by a growl coming from her own stomach, and she pretended to pout as Addie took her turn laughing.

"On second thought, maybe we ought to call down and have something sent up," Clara said. "I wouldn't want you to lose your strength."

"That's very generous of you," Addie said, grinning.

"Oh, I'm not that generous. You're still picking up the check."

"That's only fair," Addie agreed.

"With the best wine. And appetizers and dessert," Clara added.

"Nothing but the best for my girl," Addie promised.

She was rewarded with Clara's smile, less shy but just as sweet as the day they'd met. The sight of it hadn't lost its power over her, and she didn't think it ever would.

About the Author

Cassidy Crane lives in New England with her wife and their two feline overlords. She is a librarian by day and an avid reader, crafter, sports fan, and cat servant by night. She loves hearing from readers at cassidycraneauthor@gmail.com. .

Books Available From Bold Strokes Books

An Extraordinary Passion by Kit Meredith. An autistic podcaster must decide whether to take a chance on her polyamorous guest and indulge their shared passion, despite her history. (978-1-63679-679-6)

Heart's Appraisal by Jo Hemmingwood. Andy and Hazel can't deny their attraction, but they'll never agree on the place they call home. (978-1-63679-856-1)

That's Amore by Georgia Beers. The romantic city of Rome should inspire Lily's passion for writing, if she can look away from Marina Troiani, her witty, smart, and unassumingly beautiful Italian tour guide. (978-1-63679-841-7)

Through Sky and Stars by Tessa Croft. Can Val and Nicole's love cross space and time to change the fate of humanity? (978-1-63679-862-2)

Uncomplicate It by Kel McCord. When an office attraction threatens her career, Hollis Reed's carefully laid plans demand revision. (978-1-63679-864-6)

The Unexpected Heiress by Cassidy Crane. When a cynical opportunist meets a shy but spirited heiress, the last thing she plans is for her heart to get involved. (978-1-63679-833-2)

Vanguard by Gun Brooke. Beth Wild, Subterranean freedom fighter, is in the crosshairs when she fights for her people and risks her heart for loving the exacting Celestial dissident leader, LaSierra Delmonte. (978-1-63679-818-9)

Wild Night Rising by Barbara Ann Wright. Riding Harleys instead of horses, the Wild Hunt of myth is once again unleashed upon the world. Their ousted leader and a fey cop must join forces to rein in the ride of terror. (978-1-63679-749-6)

A Thousand Tiny Promises by Morgan Lee Miller. When estranged childhood friends Audrey and Reid reunite to fulfill their best friend's dying wish, the last thing they expect is a journey toward healing their broken friendship and discovering a newfound love for each other. (978-1-63679-630-7)

Behold My Heart by Ronica Black. Alora Anders is a highly successful artist who's losing her vision. Devastated, she hires Bodie Banks, a young struggling sculptor, as a live-in assistant. Can Alora open her mind and her heart to accept Bodie into her life? (978-1-63679-810-3)

Fearless Hearts by Radclyffe. One wounded woman, one determined to protect her—and a summertime of risk, danger, and desire. (978-1-63679-837-0)

Stranger in the Sand by Renee Roman. Grace Langley is haunted by guilt. Fagan Shaw wishes she could remember her past. Will finding each other bring the closure they're looking for in order to have a brighter future? (978-1-63679-802-8)

The Nursing Home Hoax by Shelley Thrasher and Ann Faulkner. In this fresh take for grown-ups on the classic Nancy Drew series, crime-solving duo Taylor and Marilee investigate suspicious activity at a small East Texas nursing home. (978-1-63679-806-6)

The Rise and Fall of Conner Cody by Chelsey Lynford. A successful yet lonely Hollywood starlet must decide if she can let go of old wounds and accept a chance at family, friendship, and the love of a lifetime. (978-1-63679-739-7)

A Conflict of Interest by Morgan Adams. Tensions rise when a one-night stand becomes a major conflict of interest between an up-and-coming senior associate and a dedicated cardiac surgeon. (978-1-63679-870-7)

A Magnificent Disturbance by Lee Lynch. These everyday dykes and their friends will stop at nothing to see the women's clinic thrive and, in the process, their ideals, their wounds, and a steadfast allegiance to one another make them heroes. (978-1-63679-031-2)

Big Corpse on Campus by Karis Walsh. When University Police Officer Cappy Flannery investigates what looks like a clear-cut suicide, she discovers that the case—and her feelings for librarian Jazz—are more complicated than she expected. (978-1-63679-852-3)